Le Grand Meaulnes

By

Alain-Fournier

Translation by Jennifer Hashmi

CW01497557

Foreword

Henri Alban Fournier, or Alain-Fournier, was born October 3rd 1886 in La Chapelle-d'Angillon in the Cher region of France. Like the narrator of his novel, "Le Grand Meaulnes", he was the son of a school-teacher. He was killed at the beginning of the 1st World War on September 22nd 1914. He had written poems and stories which were later published under the title "Miracles", but had time for only the one novel. Many authors would sacrifice all their novels to have written "Le Grand-Meaulnes". It is the work of genius and from the beginning has had an important place among French classics. From the time that it was published in 1913 readers were intrigued to learn if Augustin Meaulnes' meeting with Yvonne de Gallais was autobiographical. In the nature of literature it was partly autobiographical, but on his own meeting with Yvonne de Quievrecourt he built a majestic work of the imagination unlike anything to be found anywhere else in the literature of the world. Augustin Meaulnes was not Alain-Fournier. Nor probably was Yvonne de Gallais Yvonne de Quievrecourt. Nor is this simply a love story. In this book Alain-Fournier managed to put down on paper the nature of nostalgia, the regret for things long since past and lament that certain things had not been done differently, the pain of loss of that which can never be regained. Readers may never have seen Meaulnes' lost manor, or met the de Gallais family, or Francois Seurel, or Augustin's boyhood friends, but in their story is an echo of the universal experience of those who look back to a time in their youth when there seemed to be all sorts of possibilities which were never realized, and to a period of innocence when it seemed possible to make the world a happy place.

The book is not all about pain and loss. Seurel's recollections of his parents and their family life, and his description of the other boys in his class and their foibles will find echoes in the memories of many of his readers. It is our story. We don't know the people, but we recognize what Alain-Fournier is talking about. It is a miracle that such a book could have been written by a man in his twenties.

In this translation Jennifer Hashmi has not tried to transform Le Grand Meaulnes into an English version of a French novel. At times she has found it necessary to give a literal translation of a sentence in order not to lose the flavor of the original. This has resulted on occasion in a slight awkwardness in the English syntax, but the narrative poetic style of the original has been left as far as possible intact, pointing, as it does in the French, to something just out of sight, something unattainable. Alain-Fournier communicates in nuances, hints, recollections. The meaning is hidden in the memory of Francois. The frequent use of ellipses which allow readers to fill in the gaps for themselves are preserved in order to pass on the mystery of the original text. Ms. Hashmi has thus adhered as literally as possible to the French wording to retain the intangible quality of Alain-Fournier's narrative. The word "lost" recurs many times. The story is about searching for that which is lost, and evokes the sense of yearning for lost youth, lost dreams, lost people.

On a trip to the station by horse and trap from his school in Sainte-Agathe Meaulnes loses his way and stumbles on a manor-house where all the local people are about to celebrate the return of the land-owner's son and his fiancée. The children are in fancy-dress, and a feast is prepared. The trees are decorated with lanterns and the whole estate is transformed into a magical place. Meaulnes is entranced. The adventure culminates in his meeting and talking with the most beautiful girl he has ever seen. He has to leave the manor-house at night in a carriage with a lot of villagers, and is dropped off on a main road.

On his return to school he is desperate to trace the whereabouts of the manor-house, so that he can return. His confidant is Francois Seurel, the son of the headmaster of the school. Francois too is captivated by his friend's story, but they are teenagers and they hide their secrets still like children. A clue is found at last with the arrival of a caravan of travelling players. Meaulnes recognizes the pierrot as having been present at the lost manor-house on the night of the mysterious fete. The story is about youthful idealism which before claiming any reward must first atone for whatever fault has been committed. It is about adventures and exploits, and about setting off on journeys. The goal is always just beyond the horizon.

The story is told by Francois who narrates all that he has held precious in his memory of Augustin Meaulnes, the fellow student and companion who changed his own life for ever and those of all the members of his class at Sainte-Agathe.

CONTENTS

Part 1   4

1.   The Boarder   5
2.   After Four O'Clock   11
3.   I Frequent a Basket-Maker's Shop   14
4.   The Flight   18
5.   The Carriage Returns   22
6.   A Knock at the Window   25
7.   The Silk Waistcoat   30
8.   The Adventure   35
9.   The Halt   38
10. The Sheepfold   41
11. The Mysterious Domaine   43
12. Wellington's Room   47
13. The Strange Fete   49
14. The Strange Fete (continued)   52
15. The Meeting   56
16. Frantz de Galais   62
17. The Strange Fete (conclusion)   67

Part 2

1.   The Great Game   71
2.   We Fall into an Ambush   75
3.   The Travelling Actor at School   79
4.   In which it is a Question of the Domaine   84
5.   The Man in Canvas Shoes   89
6.   A Dispute in the Wings   92

7.	The Actor Takes off his Bandage	95
8.	The Police!	98
9.	In Search of the Lost Path	100
10.	The Washing	106
11.	I Betray	109
12.	Meaulnes' Three Letters	112

Part 3

1.	The Bathing	118
2.	At Florentin's	123
3.	An Apparition	130
4.	The Great News	136
5.	The Picnic Party	141
6.	The Picnic Party (conclusion)	146
7.	The Wedding Day	152
8.	The Call of Frantz	155
9.	The Happy People	159
10.	Frantz's House	163
11.	Conversation in the Rain	168
12.	The Burden	172
13.	The Monthly Homework Exercise-Book	178
14.	The Secret	180
15.	The Secret (continued)	185
16.	The Secret (conclusion)	190

Epilogue

Part I

1.   The Boarder

He came to our home one Sunday in November 189-.

I continue to say "our home" although the house no longer belongs to us. We left the district about fifteen years ago and we shall certainly never return there.

We lived in the building of the Senior School in Sainte-Agathe. My father, whom I called M. Seurel as the other pupils did, directed both the Senior School where preparation for the primary school teachers' diploma was given, and the Middle School. My mother taught the junior class.

Imagine a long red house covered with Virginia creeper and having five French-windows, on the outskirts of the town; then a huge yard with play-grounds and a laundry opening in front through a big gate on to the village street, and on the North side a small gate opening on to the road which led to the station three kilometres away. To the South and behind there were fields, gardens and meadows which connected with suburbs…such is the plan briefly of that home where passed the most tormented and the most precious days of my life, the hope from whence our adventures departed, to return and break themselves like waves on a deserted rock.

The chance of departmental changes, a decision by the Inspector or the Prefect, took us there. Towards the end of the holidays a long time earlier, a trap which preceded our household effects had left us, my mother and myself, by a small rusty gate. Some boys who were flying kites in the garden ran away silently through the holes in the hedge…My mother whom we called Millie, and who was the most methodical manager I have ever known, had entered the rooms which were full of dusty straw, and said, as she did at every transfer, that our furniture would never fit into such a poorly constructed house…She came out to confide her despondency to me. While talking she had cleaned my face, blackened by the journey, with her handkerchief. Then she returned to calculate the number of openings which would have to be closed to make the accommodation habitable…While I, wearing a large ribboned straw hat, remained

5

outside in this strange gravel yard, poking about a little round the wall and the shed.

It is thus at least that I imagine our arrival, because immediately I try to recall the distant memory of that first evening, so full of anticipation, in our yard in Sainte-Agathe, I remember already other times of expectation. Already I see myself, both hands leaning on the bars of the gate, watching anxiously for someone who should appear along the main road, and if I try to imagine that first night I spent in my loft in the first-floor attics, already there are other nights I remember. I am no longer alone in that room; a large unquiet but friendly shadow passes along the walls and walks. All the peaceful countryside – the school , old M. Martin's field with its' three walnut trees, the garden invaded after four o'clock by visiting ladies – is forever in my memory disturbed and transformed by the presence of him who turned our adolescence upside-down and even in leaving, left us no repose.

We had been ten years in that district when Meaulnes arrived. I was fifteen years old. It was a cold Sunday in November, the first day of Autumn when there was a promise of Winter in the air. The whole day Millie had waited for the carriage from the station which was to bring her a hat for the Winter season. In the morning she had missed Mass, and until the sermon I had sat with the other children in the choir beside the bells watching anxiously to see her enter in her new hat..

In the afternoon I had to go to Vespers alone.

"Besides," she said to console me while brushing down my childish suit with her hand, "even if the hat had arrived I expect I would have had to spend my Sunday re-working it."

Our Winter Sundays often passed this way. From the morning my father would be far away in a small boat on the mist-enveloped pond fishing for pike, and my mother would retire to her dark room till nightfall to patch up her humble fineries. She would shut herself in thus, for fear of one of her women friends, as poor as herself but proud, coming and surprising her. And I, Vespers over, would wait, reading in the cold sitting-room, until she opened the door to show me how the work was going.

That Sunday some excitement in front of the church had kept us outside after Vespers. A baptism under the porch had attracted some boys. In the square there were several men from the town arrayed in their firemen's jerseys, standing in groups, frozen and stamping their feet. They listened to Boujardon, the brigadier, tangling himself up in drill.

The baptism bell stopped abruptly like the chimes for a fete when there has been a mistake about the day and the place. Boujardon and his men, their equipment slung across their shoulders, removed their pump at a gentle trot, and I saw them disappear at the first turning followed by four silent boys snapping the twigs along the frozen road with their heavy boots, as they went where I dared not follow.

In the town there was no longer anything alive except Daniel's café where I could hear the muffled discussions, now louder, now softer, of the drinkers. And brushing against the low wall of the great yard which separated our house from the village, I arrived, worried about my delay, at the little gate.

It was half open and I saw immediately that something unusual was happening.

By the dining-room window, the nearest of the five French-windows, a woman with grey hair was bending over, trying to see through the curtains. She was small and wore a black old-fashioned velvet bonnet. She had thin delicate features, ravaged however by anxiety, and I don't know for what apprehension, but the sight of her checked me at the first step in front of the gate.

"Where has he gone?" she was saying under her breath. "My God, he was with me just now. He's already done a tour of the house. Maybe he's run away...."

And between each phrase she gave three small barely audible taps on the window-pane.

No-one came to open the door to the unknown visitor. Millie no doubt had received the hat from the station and was unable to hear anything from inside the red room. Beside a bed strewn with old ribbons and limp feathers she would be stitching, unpicking, and refurbishing her modest attire...And indeed when I entered the dining-room followed by the visitor, my mother emerged, trying with both hands to balance wires, threads, ribbons and feathers on her head...She smiled at me, her blue eyes tired from having worked till dusk, and exclaimed,

"Look! I was waiting to show you..."

But seeing the woman seated in the big armchair on the other side of the room she stopped disconcerted. Quickly she removed her hat and throughout the scene which followed held it reversed like a nest against her chest with her right hand over it.

The woman in the bonnet who was holding an umbrella, and a leather bag between her knees, had begun to explain herself, wagging her head slightly and clicking her tongue like a lady on a visit. She had recovered all her aplomb. She had even, while speaking of her son, a superior and mysterious air which intrigued us.

They had both come by coach from La Ferte-d'Angillon forty kilometers from Sainte-Agathe. She was a widow and very rich from what we could understand. She had lost the younger of her two children, Antoine, who had died one evening on his return from school as a result of bathing in a contaminated pond. She had decided to put the older brother, Augustin, as a boarder in our school to take the Senior School course.

And immediately she fell into a eulogy of this boarder she had brought to us. I could no longer recognize the grey-haired woman bent in front of the door of a minute earlier, imploring and haggard like a hen which seems to have lost a wild bird from its' brood.

What she recounted with such admiration about her son was very surprising. He liked to please her and often he would follow the banks of the river, bare-legged, to bring her eggs from the water-hens and wild duck hidden in the gorse...He also set fish-traps...The other night he had discovered a pheasant in the wood caught in a snare...

I who dared not return home when I had a tear in my shirt looked at Millie in astonishment.

But my mother was no longer listening. She signaled to the woman to be quiet, and placing her nest carefully on the table she rose silently as if going to surprise someone....

And above us in fact in the tiny room where the dusty trappings of the last fourteenth of July* were piled up, an unknown but assured

---

* The fourteenth of July is the date of the falling of the Bastille during the

8

step strode back and forth shaking the ceiling. It crossed the length of the dark attics on the first floor, and was lost eventually in the area of some unused adjoining rooms where we put limes to dry and apples to ripen.

"Even earlier I heard that noise in the downstairs rooms," said Millie quietly, "and I thought it was you Francois who had returned..."

No-one replied. We were all three standing, our hearts thumping, when the attic door leading on to the kitchen steps opened. Someone came down the steps, crossed the kitchen and appeared in the darkened entrance to the dining-room.

"Is that you Augustin?" said the woman.

It was a big boy of about seventeen. At first in the deepening twilight I could not see more of him than a peasant's felt hat worn on the back of his head, and his black shirt belted at the waist as students wear them. I could also make out that he was smiling...He saw me, and before anyone could ask him for an explanation said,

"Are you going into the yard?"

I hesitated a second. Then, as Millie didn't stop me, I put on my cap and went towards him. We went out by the kitchen door into the playground which was already enveloped in dusk. By the light which was still left I noted as we walked his angular face, straight nose, and his downy lip.

"Well," he said, "I found this in your attic. You've never looked there."

He held in his hand a small wheel of blackened wood with a string of partly burnt squibs round it. It must have been the sun or the moon from the fireworks left from the fourteenth of July.

"Two of them have not been set off. We can still light them," he said tranquilly with the air of one who hopes to find even better ones later.

He threw his hat on the ground and I saw that his hair was close-cropped like a peasant's. He showed me the two fuses with the ends of their wicks in the paper, which the flame had eaten into,

---

Revolution of 1789. It is a national holiday in France and is celebrated with fireworks and bonfires.

blackened, and then abandoned. He planted the hub of the wheel in the sand and took from his pocket (to my great astonishment for these were strictly forbidden to us) a box of matches. Bending carefully he set light to the wick. Then, taking my hand, he pulled me quickly back.

A moment later, my mother who was coming out on to the doorstep with Meaulnes' mother after having discussed and fixed the boarding charge, saw two showers of red and white stars shoot up on the playground with the sound of air from bellows; and for the space of a second she could see me dressed in the magic light, holding the hand of the big new boy and not flinching...

This time she dared not say anything.

And that evening at dinner there was at the family table a silent companion who ate, his head low, undisturbed by the eyes of the three of us fixed on him.

2. After Four O'clock

Until that time I had hardly ever run about in the streets with the boys of the town. A disease of the hip from which I suffered till about the year 189- had made me timid and melancholy. I can see myself now following the lively schoolboys in the lanes which surrounded the house hopping miserably on one leg.

I was hardly allowed to go out even, and I remember Millie who was very proud of me bringing me back home with sharp cuffs after meeting me jumping on one foot with the village ruffians.

The arrival of Augustin Meaulnes which coincided with my recovery marked the beginning of a new life.

Before his arrival, when school finished at four o'clock, a long evening of solitude stretched before me. My father would carry the fire from the stove in the classroom to the fire-place in our dining-room, and gradually the last of the lingering boys would abandon the cold school-room, where eddies of smoke hung in the air.

There would be some more games and racing in the yard and then night would fall. The two pupils who had swept the classroom would look in the shed for their caps and capes and leave quickly, their bags in their arms, through the open main gate...

Then as long as there was a glimmer of light I would be In the Town Hall archives room, full of dead flies and notices flapping in the wind, and I would read, seated in an old rocking-chair by the window which looked out on to the garden.

When it was dark and the dogs of the neighbouring farms began to howl and there was a light in the window of our small kitchen I would return home. My mother would have begun to prepare the meal. I would climb three steps of the staircase to the attic and sit there without saying anything, my head leaning against the cold bars of the hand-rail, watching her light the fire in that narrow kitchen where the flame of a candle flickered...

But someone had come who had lifted me out of all those peaceful pleasures of childhood. Someone had snuffed out the candle which lit up for me the sweet maternal face bent over the evening

11

meal. Someone had extinguished the lamp around which we had been a happy family every night after my father had latched the wooden shutters across the French-windows. And the one who did that was Augustin Meaulnes whom the other pupils soon called big Meaulnes.

From the time that he was a boarder with us, that is to say the first day of December, the school ceased to be deserted in the evenings after four o'clock. In spite of the cold in the classroom from the swinging doors, and protests from the sweepers with their buckets of water, after school there were always about twenty boys, as many from the countryside as from the town, grouped around Meaulnes. And there would be long discussions and interminable disputes, into the middle of which I would slip, nervous and happy.

Meaulnes would say nothing, but it was for his benefit that some of the more talkative boys would advance to the middle of the group and tell some long story about poaching, calling his companions in turn as witnesses. They would support him noisily and the others would listen, mouths open, and laughing silently

Seated on a desk and swinging his legs Meaulnes would be lost in thought. At the exciting parts he would laugh also, but moderately, as if reserving his own shouts of laughter for some better story known to him alone. Then as night fell, when the light through the window-panes of the classroom no longer illuminated the confused group of young people, Meaulnes would get up suddenly, and breaking through the close circle, would cry,

"Come on, let's go!"

Then everyone would follow him and their shouts would be heard disappearing into the darkness at the top of the town...

Now I too had begun to accompany them. With Meaulnes I would go to the doors of the stables on the outskirts of the town at the time when the cows were being milked...We would enter the shops, and in the darkness between two clacks of his trade the weaver would shout,

"Here are the students!"

Generally by dinner-time we would find ourselves near the main road where Desnoues, the wheelwright, who was also the black-smith, lived. His shop was an ancient inn with big double flap-doors left open. From the road the grating of the bellows of the forge could be heard, and in the ringing darkness we could see by the light of the brazier country people who had stopped their carts for a while to chat, or sometimes a student like ourselves leaning in the doorway and watching without saying anything.

And it was there that everything began about eight days before Christmas.

3. I Frequent a Basket-Maker's Shop

Rain had fallen all day and did not stop till evening. The day had been mortally dull. At recreation time no-one went out, and my father, M. Seurel, kept shouting in class.

"Don't shuffle your feet like that boys!"

After the last recreation of the day, or as we used to say, after the last "quarter-hour", M. Seurel who had been walking up and down thoughtfully for a while stopped and struck the table sharply with a large ruler. The restless murmur of the end of a school day was quietened, and in the attentive silence he said,

"Who will go tomorrow in the carriage with Francois to meet M. and Mme Charpentier from the station?"

These were my grandparents. Grandfather Charpentier was an old retired forest guard and wore a great grey woolen hooded cloak and a rabbit fur cap he called his kepi. The small boys knew him well. In the mornings he would take a bucket of water to wash his face, and splash after the fashion of old soldiers, rubbing his short pointed beard absently. A circle of children, their hands behind their backs, would watch him with respectful curiosity…And they also knew my Grandmother Charpentier, a small peasant woman with a knitted cap, because Millie used to bring her at least once into the smallest children's class.

Every year, a few days before Christmas, we would go to the station to meet them from the two minutes past four train. To visit us they had crossed the whole department carrying bundles of chestnuts wrapped in napkins. As soon as they had stepped over the threshold of our house, muffled up and a little hesitant, we'ld would close all the doors for them, and this would mark the beginning of a grand week of festivities for us.

To drive the carriage with me to go and fetch them, a sensible companion was needed. He had to be someone who would not overturn us into the ditch, and a little urbane also because Grandfather swore easily and Grandmother was a bit talkative.

At M. Seurel's question a dozen voices were raised at the same time.

"Big Meaulnes! Big Meaulnes!" But M. Seurel pretended not to hear. Then they shouted,

"Fromentin!"

And others,

"Jasmin Delouche!"

The youngest of the boys who used to ride in the fields at full gallop on his sow, cried in a piercing voice,

"Me! Me!"

Dutremblay and Moucheboeuf contented themselves with raising their hands timidly.

I would have liked Meaulnes. This little trip in the donkey-trap would have become a more important event. He wanted it too but he affected a disdainful silence. All the older pupils were sitting like him on the table with their feet on the bench as we used to do during periods of relaxation or excitement. Coffin, his shirt rolled up round his waist embraced the iron pole which supported the beam of the classroom, and began to climb it in his elation. But M. Seurel quelled everyone by saying

"Alright. It will be Moucheboeuf."

And we all went back in silence to our places.

At four o'clock in the great icy yard grooved by the rain I found myself alone with Meaulnes. We were both looking silently towards the town, shining after the rain but drying in the wind. Soon young Coffin came out of his house wearing a hood and holding a piece of bread in his hand. Keeping close to the walls he arrived eventually, whistling, at the wheelwright's door. Meaulnes opened the gate and called to him. The next moment we were all three installed in the warm glowing shop which was buffeted violently outside by gusts of icy wind. Coffin and I were seated next to the forge, our muddy feet in the white shavings. Meaulnes, his hands in his pockets, leaned silently against the shutters at the entrance. From time to time a village woman would pass along the road on her way from the butcher's shop, her head bent against the wind, and we would raise our heads to see who it was.

No-one said anything. The blacksmith and his labourer, one blowing the forge, the other beating the iron, threw great rude shadows on the wall... remember that evening as one of the most important evenings of my adolescence. There was in me a mixture of pleasure and anxiety. I was afraid that my companion would take from me the small happiness of going to the station in the trap. Yet without daring to admit it to myself I expected of him some extraordinary enterprise which would topple us all.

From time to time the regular peaceful work of the shop would be interrupted for a moment. The blacksmith would put down his hammer with a loud resonant clang on the anvil. In his leather apron he would examine the piece of iron which he had been working. Then straightening his head and sighing heavily, he said,

"Well! And how is youth?"

The labourer, one hand on the bellows chain and his left fist on his hips, regarded us laughing. Then the muffled clanging was resumed.

During one of the pauses we saw Millie through the doors passing by in the strong wind, wrapped in a shawl and carrying small packets.

The blacksmith asked,

"Is M. Charpentier coming soon?"

"Tomorrow, I said, "with my Grandmother. I'm going in the trap to the station to meet them from the four two train."

"In Fromentin's trap?"

"No, in M. Martin's," I replied quickly.

"Oh! Then you won't be back in a hurry!"

And both of them, his labourer and himself, began to laugh. The labourer raised his hand slowly to say something.

"With Fromentin's mare you could go and meet them at Vierzon. There's an hour's wait there. It's fifteen kilometers. You would have returned before Martin's donkey was even harnessed."

"That's a mare that can move," said the other.

"And I know Fromentin lends it willingly."

The conversation ended there. The shop was again a place full of sparks and bangs, and each of us was left to his own thoughts.

But when the time came for us to leave and I rose to signal to Meaulnes, he did not see me at first. Leaning on the door, his head bent, he seemed to be deeply absorbed in what had just been said. Seeing him thus, lost in thought, and looking as if through mist at those men peacefully working, I was reminded suddenly of Robinson Crusoe, that English adolescent, who used to be seen frequenting a basket-maker's shop before his great departure...

And I have often thought of it since.

4. The Flight

At two o'clock in the afternoon the next day the Senior School classroom is bright in the middle of the frozen countryside, like a ship on the ocean. One cannot smell brine or grease, as in a fishing-boat, but there is the smell of herrings grilling on the stove, and of singed wool from those who after coming in are warming themselves too close to it.

The end of the year is near so composition exercise books have been distributed. And while M. Seurel writes out problems on the board a partial silence is established, mixed with low conversation and broken by small stifled cries, and phrases of which only the first words are meant to be heard in order to frighten a neighbour, can be heard.

"Sir! Someone is..."

M. Seurel, while copying out the problems is thinking of something else. He turns round from time to time with a severe but absent-minded air. And the sly disturbance ceases completely for a second, to be reassumed again, gently at first like a hum. In the middle of this agitation I alone am quiet. Seated at the end of one of the tables for the youngest children near the windows, I have only to straighten up a little to see the garden, the stream in the woods, and then the fields.

From time to time I raise myself on my toes and look anxiously towards the Belle-Etoile farm. Since the beginning of the class I have observed that Meaulnes has not returned after the mid-day recreation. His neighbour at the table must have noticed also. Preoccupied with his composition he has not said anything yet. But as soon as he raises his head the news spreads throughout the class, and someone as usual does not miss the opportunity to exclaim aloud the first words of the phrase,

"Sir! Meaulnes..."

I know that Meaulnes has gone. More exactly I suspect him of running away. As soon as lunch was finished he must have jumped the little wall and slipped away across the fields to the Belle-Etoile, crossing the stream by the old plank...He would have asked for the mare to go and meet M. and Mme. Charpentier. He would be harnessing the mare at this moment.

The Belle-Etoile lower down on the other side of the stream is on the slope of a hill. It is a big farm whose elms and oaks in the farmyard, and quickset hedge, give shade in the Summer. It is situated by a little lane which at one end joins the road to the station, and at the other end meets the suburbs of the district. Surrounded by high walls and supported by buttresses whose bases are submerged in manure, this great feudal building in the month of June is buried under leaves. From the school at nightfall one can hear the rumble of the carts and the cries of the cowherd. But today through the window I can see the high greyish wall of the yard through the bare trees, and the open gate and then through the trunks of the hedge, parallel to the stream, a ribbon of lane whitened by the frost, which leads to the station.

Nothing moves yet in the clear wintry countryside. Nothing has changed yet.

Here M. Seurel finishes copying out the second problem. Usually he gives three. If by chance today he should give only two...He would climb back on to his chair immediately and discover the absence of Meaulnes. He would send two boys to look for him in the town, and they would certainly come upon him before the mare was harnessed...

M. Seurel, the second problem copied, lets his tired arm drop for a moment. Then, to my great relief, he begins another line of writing, saying,

"This one now is more than a child's game!"

...Two small black points passing the wall of the Bell-Etoile must be the two shafts standing up from the carriage. They have disappeared. I am sure now that preparations are being made below for the departure of Meaulnes. Here is the mare appearing now, its head and chest visible between the two pilasters at the entrance. Then it stops while someone no doubt fixes a second seat behind the carriage for the passengers Meaulnes is claiming he has to bring. At last the whole equipage comes slowly out of the yard, disappears behind the hedge, and then continues at the same leisurely pace along the white lane which I can see between two broken pieces of the fence. I can recognize also in the black form holding the reins, one elbow resting carelessly on the side of the carriage in the manner of a peasant, my companion, Augustin Meaulnes.

A moment later it all disappears behind the hedge. Two men standing near the gate of the Belle-Etoile to watch the departure of the carriage are consulting each other now with increasing animation. Now one of them decides to put his hands to his mouth to call to Meaulnes and then to run a few steps along the lane in his direction. But in the carriage which has slowly reached the road to the station and will no longer be visible from the lane Meaulnes' attitude suddenly changes. One foot on the front, and sitting erect like the driver of a Roman chariot, shaking the reins with both hands, he puts his animal to full gallop, and in a moment disappears round the other side of the hill. On the lane the man who was calling him begins to run again. The other man starts to run across the field and seems to be coming towards us.

In a few minutes, at the time when M. Seurel leaves the board and rubs his hands to remove the chalk, at the moment when three voices call out at once,

"Sir! Big Meaulnes has gone!"

the man in the blue shirt is at the door. He opens it wide suddenly and raising his cap he asks from the threshold,

"Excuse me Sir, have you authorized a pupil to ask for the carriage to go to Vierzon to meet your parents? We became suspicious..."

"Not at all!" cries M. Seurel.

And immediately there is terrible confusion in the classroom. The first three pupils near the door, normally charged with throwing stones at any goats or pigs which try to enter the yard to graze on the March Pride, rush to the door. The clatter of their hob-nailed clogs on the school flag-stones is succeeded by the muffled sound of their feet in the yard outside as they skid to the small gate which is open on to the road. All the rest of the class crowd to the windows looking on to the garden. Some climb on to the tables to get a better view...

But it is too late. Big Meaulnes has escaped...

"All the same, you will go to the station with Moucheboeuf," M. Seurel tells me. "Meaulnes doesn't know the way to Vierzon. He'll get lost at the crossroads. He won't reach the station by three o'clock."

On the doorstep of the small children's classroom Millie looks out to ask,

"Whatever is the matter?"

On the road to the town people are beginning to collect. The peasant is always there, immobile, bare-headed, hat in his hand, like someone demanding justice.

5.   The Carriage Returns

When I had brought my grandparents from the station, when after dinner, seated in front of the high chimney, they began to recount in detail all that they had done since the last holidays, I realized I was not listening to them.

The little yard gate was close to the door of the dining-room. It grated when it opened. Normally as night commenced during our country evenings I would wait secretly for the grating of the gate. It would be followed by the sound of clogs clacking or being cleaned on the doorstep, sometimes by whispering before entering. And someone would knock. It would be a neighbour, the teachers…someone perhaps who had come to provide diversion for the long evening.

Now that evening I had nothing more to hope for from outside since all those I loved were reunited in our home, yet I never ceased to listen to all the sounds of the night and to wait for someone to open the gate.

My old grandfather was there with his bushy appearance like a big Gascon shepherd, his two heavy feet placed in front of him, his stick between his legs, and leaning down to knock his pipe against his shoe. He was approving with his good moist eyes what my grandmother was saying about their journey and their hens and their neighbours, and the peasants who still had not paid their rent. But I was no longer with them.

I was imagining the rolling of the carriage which would stop suddenly in front of the gate. Meaulnes would jump down from the vehicle and come in as if nothing had happened…Or maybe he would go first to take the mare back to the Belle-Etoile, and soon I would hear his footsteps ringing in the road and the gate opening…

But nothing. Grandfather stared steadily in front of him, his eyelids flickering and drooping over his eyes with the approach of sleep. Grandmother repeated her last phrase, a little embarrassed that no-one was listening.

"Is it that boy you're worried about?" she said at last.

At the station I had in fact enquired in vain. No-one had seen anyone at Vierzon who resembled Big Meaulnes. My companion must have grown late on the way. His attempt had failed. During our return in the donkey-cart I had thought over my disappointment while Grandmother talked to Moucheboeuf. On the road, whitened by frost, the little birds swarmed around the feet of the trotting donkey. From time to time in the profound stillness of the icy afternoon the cry of a distant shepherd could be heard, or of a boy calling his companion from one clump of fir-trees to another. And each time the long cry across the deserted hillsides would make me tremble as if it had been Meaulnes' voice inviting me to follow him far away...

While I was re-living all that in my mind the time had come to go to bed. My grandfather had already gone into the red room, the sitting-room being damp and icy from having been closed since the previous Winter. The lace antimacassars had been removed from the armchairs so that he could be accommodated in them. The carpets were rolled up and breakable objects put to one side. He had placed his stick on a chair and his large shoes under an armchair and had just blown out the candle. We were standing saying goodnight before separating for the night when the sound of carriages silenced us.

There seemed to be two carriages coming at a slow trot. The pace slackened and they finally came to a halt under the dining-room window which faced out on to the road but had been blocked in.

My father had taken the lamp and without waiting opened the door which he had earlier locked. Then pushing open the gate and advancing to the edge of the steps he lifted the lamp above his head to see what was happening.

Two carriages were standing there, the horse of one tied to the back of the carriage in front. A man had jumped to the ground and was hesitating...

"Is this the town-hall?" he asked, approaching. "Could you show me the way to M. Fromentin's farm, the Belle-Etoile? I found his carriage and mare without a driver going along the road near Saint-Loup des Bois. With my lantern I could see his name and address on the plate. It was in my direction and I have brought his carriage by this route to avoid accidents, but it has made me very late all the same."

We were stupefied. My father approached and lit up the carriage with his lamp.

"There was no trace of any traveler," the man went on, "not even of a cover. The animal is tired. She is limping a little."

I approached to the front and saw with the others the lost carriage which had returned to us like a piece of wreckage washed up by the high tide, the first wreckage and perhaps the last of Meaulnes' adventure.

"If it's too far to go to M. Fromentin's I'll leave the carriage with you," said the man. "I've already lost a lot of time and my people will be worried."

My father accepted the carriage. In that way we would be able to take it back to the Belle-Etoile tonight without saying what had happened. Afterwards we would decide what to tell people in the neighbourhood and write to Meaulnes' mother. Refusing a glass of wine which we offered, the man whipped his horse.

Inside the room where we had relit the candle till we returned, and my father took the carriage to the farm, we said nothing. My grandfather said,

"So then, has the traveler returned?"

The women consulted each other silently for a second.

"Yes. He has been with his mother. Now go to sleep. Don't worry."

"Ah well. So that's alright. It's just what I thought," he said.

And satisfied, he extinguished his candle and turned over in his bed to go to sleep.

This was the explanation which we gave to the people of the town. As for the mother of the fugitive it was decided to wait before writing to her. And we kept our anxiety to ourselves for three long days. I can see my father still, returning from the farm around eleven o'clock, his moustache wet with the night frost, discussing it angrily with Millie in a low anguished voice...

6.   A Knock at the Window

The fourth day was one of the coldest that Winter. From early morning the first arrivals warmed themselves by sliding around the well. They were waiting for the stove to be lit in the school before rushing to it.

Behind the gate several of us were watching for the arrival of the boys from the rural areas. They would arrive dazzled from having crossed the frost-whitened country-side and gazing at frozen ponds and the copses where the hares scampered....There was a smell of hay and stables in their clothes which made the atmosphere of the classroom heavy when they placed themselves round the red stove. And that morning one of them had brought in a basket a frozen squirrel which he had found on the road. He tried, I remember, to hang up the long-stiffened animal on a post in the shed...

Then the heavy Winter class began...

A sharp knock on the window made us raise our heads. Standing erect outside the door was big Meaulnes shaking off the frost from his shirt, his head high and looking as if dazzled!

The two pupils on the bench nearest the door rushed to open it. At the door there was some sort of private consultation which we couldn't hear, and the fugitive decided at last to enter the school.

The gust of fresh air which came in from the deserted yard, the wisps of straw which we could easily see stuck to big Meaulnes' clothes, and above all his air of a traveler who has returned tired and hungry, but spell-bound, caused in us a strange mixture of pleasure and curiosity.

M. Seurel had come down the two steps from his small desk and was giving us a dictation, and Meaulnes walked towards him in an aggressive manner. I remember how handsome he looked at that moment, my big companion, in spite of his exhausted appearance and his eyes red from having spent the nights outside no doubt.

He went towards the chair and said in the assured tone of one who is reporting a piece of information,

"I am back Sir."

"So I see," replied M. Seurel, looking at him curiously..."Go and take your place."

The boy turned towards us, his back a little bent and a mocking smile on his face as big indisciplined boys have when they are punished, and seizing with one hand the end of the table he slid on to his bench.

"You will take a book which I will show you," said the Master – all heads were turned towards Meaulnes - "while your friends finish their dictation."

And the class went on as before. From time to time big Meaulnes turned towards me. Then he would look through the window to where the garden lay white, fleecy, and still, and to the deserted fields where sometimes a crow would alight. In the classroom the heat was oppressive round the red stove. My friend, his head in his hands, began to read. I saw that after commencing twice his eyelids closed. I knew he was going to sleep.

"I would like to go to bed Sir," he said, raising his hand a little. "I haven't slept for three nights."

"Go then," said M. Seurel, wishing above all to avoid an incident.

All heads were raised; all pens poised in mid-air, while regretfully we watched him leave, his shirt crumpled and his shoes covered with earth.

How slowly the morning went by! As mid-day approached we heard the traveler in the attic above getting ready to descend. At lunch time I found him again waiting in front of the fire close to my grandparents who were struck dumb, until at two strokes of the clock the senior pupils and the younger ones scattered in the snowy yard, and slipped like shadows past the dining-room door.

Of that lunch I can remember only a long embarrassed silence. Everything was frozen – the oiled American cloth without a table-cloth, the cold wine in the glasses, the red floor on which our feet rested...t had been decided not to push him to revolt, to ask nothing of the fugitive. And he profited from this truce by saying not a word.

At last, the desert finished, we could both run in the yard. That school-yard in the afternoon when our clogs had removed the snow....the blackened schoolyard when the thaw causes drops of water to fall from the roof of the shed...that yard full of joy and piercing cries! Meaulnes and I ran close to the walls of the building. Already two or three of our friends from the town had left the others and run up to us with cries of joy, making the mud splash under their clogs, their hands in their pockets and scarves hanging loose. But my companion ran into the classroom where I followed him, and closed the door just in time to check the assault of those behind us. There was a violent clatter of shaking glass, and the sound of clogs stamping on the steps. One push made the iron shaft yield and then the two flaps of the door would have opened but already Meaulnes, at the risk of cutting himself on its' broken ring, had turned the small key which locked the door.

We used to consider such conduct annoying. In Summer those who were locked out this way used to run round into the garden, and often managed to climb in through a window before they could all be closed. But this was December and they were already all closed. For a moment outside they pushed at the door shouting insults at us. Then one by one they turned their backs and went away, heads bent and readjusting their scarves. In the classroom which smelt of sweet chestnuts and wine there were only the two sweepers who were moving the tables. I went to the stove to warm myself idly until afternoon class, while Augustin Meaulnes searched in the Master's desk and in the other desks. He soon discovered a small atlas which he began to study passionately, standing on the dais, his head between his hands.

I was starting to go to him. I would have put my hand on his shoulder and we would have followed together no doubt on the map the direction which he had taken, but the communicating door from the junior classroom was suddenly violently pushed open, and Jasmin Delouche followed by a boy from the town and three others from the country surged in with a shout of triumph. One of the junior class windows had probably not been properly closed. They must have pushed it open and jumped through.

Jasmin Delouche, although still quite small, was one of the older boys in the Senior School. He was very jealous of big Meaulnes although he pretended to be his friend. Before the arrival of our boarder it had been he, Delouche, who was the leader of the class. He had a pale, rather insignificant face, and oiled hair. He was the only son of widow Delouche, the inn-keeper, and he liked to play the man. He would repeat boastfully what he had heard said by the gamblers and vermouth drinkers.

At his entrance Meaulnes raised his head, frowning, as the boys rushed in, pushing each other to the stove.

"One can't have a minute's peace here!" he cried.

"If you aren't happy here you should have stayed where you were," replied Jasmin Delouche without raising his head, feeling himself to be supported by his companions.

I think that Augustin was in that state of fatigue when anger arises and surprises everyone before it can be contained.

"You," he said straightening up and closing his book, "can begin by leaving this room."

The other sniggered.

"Oh!" he cried, "because you escaped for three days you think you are going to be master now?"

Then associating others in his quarrel, he said,

"You can't make us go out you know!"

But Meaulnes was already on to him and there was a struggle, the sleeves of their shirts coming unstitched with a cracking sound, but Martin, one of the boys from the countryside, intervened on Jasmin's behalf.

"You let him go!" he cried, nostrils distended and shaking his head like a ram.

With a violent push Meaulnes threw him, reeling, and arms spread, into the middle of the classroom. Then he caught Jasmin by the neck with one hand, and opening the door with the other he tried to throw him outside. Jasmin caught hold of the tables and dragged his feet on the flags making his hob-nails grate. Martin having regained his balance returned to the fray, his head ducked forwards and furious. Meaulnes let go of Jasmin to deal with the imbecile and would have found himself in difficulties perhaps, but the inner door half opened, M. Seurel appeared, his head turned back towards the kitchen as he finished a conversation with someone before entering.

Immediately the battle ceased. The remainder of the boys huddled round the stove, heads down, having avoided to the end taking any part. Meaulnes sat in his place, his sleeve torn and crumpled. As for the infuriated Jasmin, in the few seconds before the strike of the ruler for the start of the class, he could be heard saying,

"He can't stand teasing any more. He's a show-off. He thinks we don't know where he's been!"

"Fool!" said Meaulnes in the silence which had already fallen. "I don't even know myself where I've been."

Then shrugging his shoulders, his head in his hands, he began to learn his lessons.

7. The Silk Waistcoat

Our bedroom was, as I have said, a large attic, half attic half room. It had windows into the adjoining rooms, but for some reason this one was lit by a dormer window. It was impossible to close the door completely because it stuck on the floor. Each time we went upstairs in the evening we had to screen the candle with our hand to protect it from the draughts of air which threatened it in that big house. Each time we would try to close the door but each time we were obliged to give up. And the whole night we would feel around us, penetrating into our room, the silence of the three attics It was there where we found ourselves, Augustin and myself, that same Winter's evening.

While I had undressed quickly and tossed my clothes in a heap on the chair, my companion began to undress silently. From the iron bedstead with its' cretonne curtains with a vine-stalk pattern, into which I had already climbed, I watched him. In a while he stood up and started walking back and forth as he undressed. The candle which he had placed on the wicker table, woven by gypsies, threw on the wall his wandering towering shadow.

Quite unlike me he folded and arranged his student's clothes carefully, but in a bitter distracted manner. I watched him place his heavy belt on the chair, and fold on its back his black, creased, and dirty shirt, and lean over, his back towards me, to spread it over the foot of the bed…but when he straightened up and turned towards me I saw that he wore in place of the leather-buttoned waistcoat which was part of the uniform under the jacket, a strange silk waistcoat. It was very open and was fastened low down by a close row of little mother-of-pearl buttons.

It was a garment of charming fantasy like young people used to wear when they danced with our grandmothers in the balls of 1830*.

I remember now the great peasant-student standing bare-headed, for he had put his cap carefully with his other clothes, his face so young, and looking so valiant and tough already. He had begun his

---

* Balls celebrating the coronation of Louis Philippe after the Revolution

pacing across the room again when he began to unbutton the mysterious item of costume which was not his own. And it was strange to see him in his shirt-sleeves with his trousers which were too short and his muddy shoes, putting his hand on the waistcoat of a marquis.

As soon as he touched it he came abruptly out of his reverie and turned his head towards me, regarding me with an anxious eye. I had a slight desire to laugh. He smiled along with me and his face cleared.

"Oh," I said, emboldened, in a low voice, "where did you get that from?"

But his smile was immediately extinguished. He passed his heavy hand a couple of times over his shaved hair, and then suddenly, like one who can no longer resist his desire, he put on his jacket again and buttoned it firmly over his fine waistcoat, and then his crumpled shirt......Finally he sat on the edge of his bed, slipping off his shoes which fell noisily to the floor, dressed like a soldier on the alert in his billet. Then he stretched out on his bed and blew out his candle.

Towards the middle of the night I woke suddenly. Meaulnes was standing in the middle of the room, his cap in his hand,, and he was looking for something in his portmanteau – a cloak which he put round his back....the room was very dark...not even the clarity which the reflection from snow sometimes gives. An icy wind blew across the dead garden and over the roof.

I sat up a little and cried in a low voice,

"Meaulnes! You're going again?"

He did not reply. Then suddenly mad, I said,

"Alright I'll go with you. You'll have to take me too."

And I jumped out of bed. He came to me and seized me by the arm, forcing me to sit on the edge of the bed, and said to me,

"I can't take you Francois. If I knew my way well you would come. But first I have to find it on the map, and so far I haven't succeeded."

"Then even you can't go again."

"You're right. It's useless…," he said, discouraged. "Alright, go back to bed. I promise not to go again without you."

31

And he began again his pacing up and down the room. I dare not say anything more to him. He walked, stopped, and walked again more quickly like someone who searches mentally for something, or relives memories, confronts them, compares them, calculates, and suddenly believes he has recovered them; then loses the thread and starts again to search...

That wasn't the only night when wakened by the sound of his step I found him thus about one o'clock in the morning, walking across the room and the attics – like sailors who can't break the habit of keeping the watch, and get up in the middle of the night in the depths of their Bretton homesteads and dress at their habitual hour to survey the night on land.

Two or three times during the month of January, and the first fortnight of February, I was dragged thus from my sleep. Big Meaulnes was standing there dressed, his cloak on his back, ready to leave, and each time on the threshold of this mysterious land from which he had escaped once already, he stopped, hesitated. On the point of lifting the lock of the staircase door and of slipping out through the kitchen door which he could easily have opened without anyone hearing, he drew back once again...Then, during the long middle hours of the night he would pace up and down again feverishly, deep in thought, in the abandoned attics.

Finally one night about the fifteenth of February he woke me by placing his hand gently on my shoulder.

The day had been very turbulent. Meaulnes, who had completely abandoned his games with his old comrades, had remained through the last recreation of the evening, seated on a bench, occupied with working out a mysterious little map, following it with his finger, and studying for a long time in an atlas the region of the Cher. There was an incessant coming and going between the yard and the classroom. The clogs were noisy as boys chased each other from table to table jumping over the benches and the platform in one leap...They knew it was not wise to go near Meaulnes when he was thus engaged. Meanwhile as the recreation progressed, two or three boys from the town, as if in play, crept up to him silently, and looked over his shoulder. One of them went so far as to push the others on to

Meaulnes. He closed the atlas quickly, hid his paper, and seized the last of the three boys while the others escaped.

…It was the surly Ciraudat who adopted a whimpering tone and tried to kick with his feet. In the end he was pushed outside by big Meaulnes at whom he shouted angrily,

"Big coward! I'm not surprised they're all against you and want to fight you!" and a volley of insults followed to which we responded without having heard exactly what he was trying to say. It was I who shouted loudest for I had taken the side of big Meaulnes. There was a sort of pact between us. The promise he had given me to take me with him, without saying, as everyone else did, that 'I wouldn't be able to walk" had bound me to him for ever. I never ceased to think of his mysterious journey. I was persuaded that he had met a young girl. She was certainly much more beautiful than the other girls of the district, more beautiful than Jeanne whom one could see in the nuns' garden through the keyhole, or blond pink Madeleine the baker's daughter, or Jenny the chatelaine's daughter who was admirable but mad and kept locked up. It was certainly of a young girl that he thought in the night, like the heroes in romances. I had decided bravely to speak to him about it the next time he woke me up…

The evening after that fight, after four o'clock, we were both busy bringing in the garden tools when we heard a shout in the road. It was a band of young men and ruffians marching along in a column, four abreast, like a well-organised Company led by Delouche, Daniel, Ciraudat, and one other I didn't know. They saw us and booed vociferously. Thus all the town was against us, and preparing I don't know what war game from which we were excluded.

Meaulnes without a word put the spade and mattock which he was carrying back in the shed…But at midnight I felt his hand on my shoulder and I woke with a start.

"Get up," he said, "we'll go."

"Do you know the whole way now?"

"I know a good part of it. And we'll just have to find the rest!" he said, grinding his teeth.

"Listen Meaulnes," I said, sitting up, "Listen to me. There's only one thing for us to do. We must go together in the daylight, using your map as far as it will take us."

"It is a long way from here."

"Alright we'll go in the Summer as soon as the days are long enough."

There was a prolonged silence in which I sensed that he had accepted.

"Since we shall be going together to find the girl you love Meaulnes," I added at last, "tell me who she is. Tell me about her."

He sat at the foot of my bed. I saw his head bent in the darkness, his elbows on his knees. Then he let out a long sigh like someone who has had a heavily burdened heart for a long time and is going to confide his secret.

8.   The Adventure

My companion did not tell me all that had happened to him on the journey that night. And even after he had decided to confide everything to me, during the days of distress of which I will speak, it remained the great secret of our adolescence. But now that everything is over, now that there remains no more than dust, I can recount the strange adventure.

At half past one in the afternoon on the road to Vierzon which was by this time icy, Meaulnes made his horse go briskly because he knew he was not early. At first he amused himself only at the thought of our surprise when he brought back M. and Mme. Charpentier in the carriage at four o'clock. For certainly at that moment he had no other intention.

Presently he became very cold and wrapped his legs in a cover which he had at first refused and which the people at the Belle-Etoile had insisted on putting in the carriage.

At two o'clock he passed through the village of La Motte. He had never been in a small village during school hours and was amused to see this one so deserted and asleep. Only occasionally a curtain would be lifted showing the head of a curious housewife.

As he left La Motte, immediately after the school-house, he hesitated between two routes, and thought he remembered that he should turn left to Vierzon. No-one was about to direct him. He set the mare off at a trot along the straighter and rougher road. He passed by a wood of fir-trees and eventually met a wagon-driver. He put his hands round his mouth and called out to ask if this was the road to Vierzon. The mare, pulling on the reins, continued to trot. The man probably did not understand what he was asking. He shouted something and made a vague gesture, and Meaulnes continued along the road.

Once more he found himself out in the frozen countryside without any break or distraction. Sometimes a magpie flew up, frightened by the carriage. The traveller had wrapped his big cover round his shoulders like a cape. Thus, with his legs stretched out, and leaning

35

on the side of the carriage, he must have dozed for some considerable time....

When, thanks to the cold which had now penetrated his cover, Meaulnes awoke he saw that the countryside had changed. There were no longer distant horizons and a great white sky, but small fields, still green, with fences. To right and left the water in the ditches ran under ice. Everything suggested the approach of a river. And between the high hedges, the way was no longer along a straight road full of ruts.

The mare for a moment ceased to trot. With a stroke of the whip Meaulnes tried to make her resume her brisk speed, but she continued to walk very slowly, and the big student, leaning over with his hands on the front of the carriage, saw that she was limping on one of her back legs. Very worried he immediately jumped to the ground.

"We'll never get to Vierzon in time for the train," he said to himself.

And he dare not pursue the more disquieting thought that perhaps he had lost his way and was no longer on the road to Vierzon.

He examined the animal's foot thoroughly and could not find any trace of a wound. The mare lifted her foot very nervously when Meaulnes wanted to touch it and pawed the ground with her heavy awkward shoe. He realized at last that she merely had a pebble in her shoe. As a boy-expert in the management of cattle he crouched down and tried to take her right foot in his left hand and place it between his knees, but he was hampered by the position of the carriage. After two attempts the mare shied away and moved forward a few metres. The step of the carriage hit his head and the wheel cut his knee. He persevered however and managed to win over the frightened animal, but the pebble was so firmly lodged that Meaulnes had to take out his peasant's knife to do it.

When he had completed his task and finally raised his head, only half-attending, and his eyes preoccupied, he saw incredulously that it was getting dark....

Anyone but Meaulnes would immediately have retraced his steps. That was the only way to avoid going further astray. But he reflected that he must now be a long way from La Motte. Besides the mare might have taken a crossroad while he was asleep. And this road must in the end lead to some village...Added to all these considerations the big boy felt as he remounted the step of the carriage, and as the animal pulled impatiently at the reins, an exasperated desire growing within him, to achieve something, and arrive somewhere, in spite of all the obstacles.

He whipped the mare which leapt and began again at a brisk trot. The darkness was increasing. Along the narrow path there was just enough space for the carriage. Sometimes a dead branch from the hedge caught in a wheel and broke with a dry crack...When it was quite dark Meaulnes thought suddenly with a heaviness of heart of the dining-room at Sainte-Agathe where by that time we must all be reunited. He was seized by anger, then pride, and then a profound joy at having thus escaped without having desired it...

9. A Halt

Suddenly the mare slackened her pace as if her foot had stumbled in the dark. Meaulnes saw her lower her head and raise it a couple of times. Then she stopped dead, her nostrils down to sniff at something. Round the feet of the animal he could hear something like the ripple of water. A stream cut across the road. In Summer it would be a ford. But at this time of the year the flow was so strong that it could not freeze and it would have been dangerous to pursue any further.

Meaulnes pulled the reins gently to draw her back a few paces, and very puzzled, stood up in the carriage. It was then that he saw between the branches a light. Two or three meadows only separated I itfromtheroad...

The student climbed down from the carriage and set the mare off backwards, talking to it to calm it and still the frightened tosses of its head.

"Come along old lady! Come along! Not much further now. We'll soon know where we have come."

And pushing open the gate into a small field which bordered the road he took the carriage through. His feet sank into the soft grass. The carriage jolted silently. His head against that of the mare's he could feel the heat of her panting breath...He took her to the end of the field and put the cover over her back. Then pushing aside some branches of the hedge behind he saw the light again and a lonely house.

Nevertheless he had to cross three fields and jump a treacherous stream into which he almost plunged with both feet...At last after a final jump down from a bank he found himself in the yard of a country house. A pig was grunting in its sty. At the sound of footsteps on the frozen ground a dog began to bark furiously.

The shutter of the door was open and the light which Meaulnes had seen was that of a fire of faggots burning in a chimney. There was no other light except that from the fire. A woman in the house got up to come to the door without seeming at all afraid. The pendulum clock at that moment struck six-thirty.

"Excuse me Madame," said the boy. "I believe I have put my foot in your chrysanthemums."

Standing with a bowl in her hand she looked at him.

"It's true," she said, "that it's so dark in the yard you can't see your way."

There was a silence during which Meaulnes stood looking at the walls of the room papered with pages from illustrated journals as in an inn, and at the table on which there was a man's hat.

"Is the owner about?" he asked, sitting down.

"He's coming," replied the woman. "He's gone to look for firewood."

"It isn't that I need him," continued the young man drawing his chair closer to the fire. "But we are several huntsmen lying in wait out there. I came to ask if you could let us have a little bread."

Big Meaulnes knew that with country people, especially in isolated farms, it is necessary to speak with a lot of discretion, and never show that one does not belong to the district.

"Bread?" she said. "We can't give you much. The baker comes every Tuesday and hasn't been today"...

Augustin who had hoped to find himself near a village was alarmed.

"The baker of which village?" he asked.

"The baker of Vieux-Nancay of course," replied the woman in astonishment.

"How far is Vieux-Nancay from here approximately?" went on Meaulnes, very anxious.

"By the road I wouldn't be able to tell you exactly, but across country it's about three and a half leagues."

And she began to tell how she had a daughter in service there who came on foot to see her every first Sunday of the month and that her employers...

But Meaulnes, completely disorientated, interrupted her to say,

"Is Vieux-Nancay the nearest town?"

"No. The nearest is Les Landes, five kilometers away. But it has no shops nor a bakery. It does have a small gathering every year at the Feast of St. Martin."

Meaulnes had never heard of Les Landes. He realized he was so far astray that it was funny. But the woman who was busy now washing her bowl on the sink stone turned round, curious herself now, and looking straight at him asked slowly,

"Are you a stranger here?"

At that moment an elderly peasant appeared at the door with an armful of wood which he threw on the hearth. The woman explained to him very loudly as if he were deaf what the young man wanted.

"Oh well that's easy," he said simply, "but come closer. You aren't getting warm."

A moment later they were both installed close to the fire-dogs, the old man breaking wood to put on the fire and Meaulnes eating a bowl of milk with bread which had been offered him. Our traveller, delighted at finding himself in this humble house after all his anxieties and thinking that his strange adventure was over, was planning already to return later with his comrades to meet these good people again. He did not know that this was merely a halt and that in a short while he would continue on his way.

He asked them presently to put him on the road to La Motte, and coming round gradually to the truth he told them that he had got separated with the carriage from the other hunters, and was now completely lost.

Then the man and woman were so insistent that he stay the night with them and leave only by daylight that Meaulnes finally accepted, and went out to look for the mare to bring her into the stable.

"Mind the holes in the track," warned the old man.

Meaulnes dare not betray that he had not come by "the track". He was on the point of asking the good man to accompany him. He hesitated a moment on the doorstep, and so great was his indecision that he almost staggered. Then he went out into the dark yard.

10. The Sheepfold

To return he had to climb back up on to the bank from which he had jumped.

Slowly and with difficulty he made his way back through the grass and water, and willow enclosures, to fetch his carriage from the back of the field where he had left it. The carriage was no longer there…Motionless he strained his ears to listen to all the sounds of the night, expecting at any moment to hear the animal's collar close by. Nothing…He walked round the field. The gate was still open and a little pushed back as if the wheel of a carriage had passed through. The mare must have escaped through it by itself.

He went a few paces out on to the road and found his feet caught in the cover which had slipped off the mare on to the ground. He concluded that the mare had run in that direction. He began to run…

Without any idea beyond the fixed and mad desire to catch his vehicle, and a prey to a panic which was close to terror he ran…Sometimes his foot stumbled in the ruts. At the turnings in the complete darkness he crashed into fences, and too exhausted to stop himself in time, he struggled against thorns, his arms outstretched, tearing his hands to protect his face. For a moment he thought he heard the sound of a carriage, but it was only the jolting of a cart passing by far away on a road to the left.…

At one point he had to stop because his knee which had been cut by the carriage step was painful and stiff. He reflected that as the mare had not escaped at full gallop he should find it before long. He told himself also that a carriage does not get so lost that one can not find it again. At last he retraced his steps, weary and angry, and hardly able to walk.

Eventually he thought he was back in the area he had left, and would soon see the light from the house he was looking for.

The hedge opened into a long path.

"This is the path the old man mentioned," thought Augustin.

And he set off along it, glad that he no longer had to jump over hedges and banks. Presently the path veered to the left and the light appeared on the right. Arriving at a crossing of paths, Meaulnes in his

41

haste to reach the poor dwelling again, unthinkingly followed a path which seemed to lead directly to it. But hardly had he taken ten steps in that direction when the light disappeared either behind a hedge or because the peasants had grown tired of waiting and had closed their shutters. Bravely the student jumped into a field and made his way across it in the direction where the light had shone a short while ago. Then jumping again over an enclosure he found himself in a new path....

Discouraged and almost at the end of his tether he decided in his despair to follow this path to the end. A hundred paces further along he found himself in a great grey meadow from where he could distinguish in the distance shadows which could be juniper trees, and a dark building in a sheltered corner of the terrain. Meaulnes moved towards it. It was only a sort of cattle-run or an abandoned sheep-fold. The door opened with a groan. The moonlight, when the strong winds chased away the clouds, passed through the chinks in the partitions. There was a powerful musty smell.

Without looking any further Meaulnes stretched out on the damp straw, his elbow on the ground and his head in his hand. After removing his belt he curled up in his shirt, his knees drawn up to his stomach. He thought then of the mare's cover which he had left in the lane, and felt so unhappy, so angry with himself that he wanted to cry...

He forced himself to think of something else. Frozen to the marrow he remembered a dream – a vision rather – that he had had as a child about which he had never spoken to anyone. One morning, instead of waking in his own room where his breeches and coat hung, he found himself in a long green room, the colour of foliage. In that place there was a radiance so sweet he almost believed he could taste it. By the first window a young girl was sewing, her back turned towards him. She seemed to be waiting for him to wake up...He had not the strength to slide out of bed and walk into this enchanted place. He fell asleep again..But the next time he swore he would get up. Tomorrow morning perhaps!....

11. The Mysterious Domaine

From dawn he began to walk again but his swollen knee was hurting him. He had to keep stopping to sit down when the pain was severe. The place where he found himself was, besides, the most desolate of the Sologne. Throughout the morning he saw only a shepherdess leading her flock on the horizon. He hailed her loudly and tried to run but she disappeared without hearing him.

He continued however to follow dejectedly in her direction. Not a roof; not a soul. Not even the cry of the curlews in the reeds of the marshes. And in the perfect solitude the December sun shone, clear and icy.

It may have been three o'clock in the afternoon when he saw at last above a wood of fir-trees the spire of a grey tower.

"Some old abandoned manor-house," he thought, "some deserted pigeon-house!"

And without increasing his speed he continued on his path. At the corner of the wood between two white posts a road appeared which Meaulnes took. He walked a few steps along it and stopped, surprised and troubled by an inexplicable emotion. He walked on, sometimes with the same weary step, the icy wind chapping his lips and suffocating him at times, and sometimes uplifted by an extraordinary contentment, a perfect tranquility which was almost intoxicating, in the certainty that his destination was attained and there was no longer anything now but happiness and hope. It was a languor like that he used to experience on the eve of the great Summer Feasts when fir-trees were placed along the roads of the town at nightfall and the view from his window was obstructed by their branches.

"Such joy," he wondered to himself, "because I have arrived at this draughty old pigeon-house full of owls!"...

And annoyed with himself he stopped to consider whether it wouldn't be better to retrace his steps and continue to the next village. He stood there reflecting for a moment, head down, when he noticed that the path had been swept in big regular curves as they used to do at home for the festivals. He was in a road like the main road of La Ferte on the morning of the Assumption!...When he saw at a bend in the road a troop of people dressed for a festival and raising the dust in the road like in the months of June he could not have been more surprised.

"Could there be a festival in such a solitary place?" he wondered.

Advancing as far as the first bend he heard the sound of voices approaching. He threw himself into the young bushy fir-trees at the side of the road and crouched down, hardly daring to breathe, to listen. They were children's voices. A group of children passed close by him. One, probably a little girl, was speaking in so wise and decided a tone, that Meaulnes, even though he could hardly understand the meaning of her words, could not help smiling.

"Only one thing worries me," she was saying, "and that's the problem of the horses. For example we can't stop Daniel climbing on the big yellow pony!"

"No-one will be able to stop me," came the mocking voice of a young boy. "Don't we have permission to do what we like? Even things which might hurt us, if we please!"...

And the voices were lost in the distance even as another group of children was already approaching.

"If the ice has melted by tomorrow morning," said a little girl, "we'll go by boat."

"But will they let us?" asked another.

"You know we are organizing the Fete as we like."

"And supposing Frantz returns this evening with his fiancée?"

"He will do what we want!"...

"It seems to be to do with a marriage," thought Meaulnes. "But do the children rule here? Strange place!"

He wanted to come out of his hiding-place to ask them where he might find food and drink. He stood up to see the last group disappearing. They were three little girls in straight knee-length dresses and they had pretty hats with strings. Each had a white feather which curved into her neck. One of them half turned as she leaned towards her companion who was explaining something, wagging her finger.

"I would frighten them," thought Meaulnes, looking down at his torn peasant's shirt and the ornamented belt he wore as a student of Sainte-Agathe.

Fearing that the children might meet him on their return he continued on his way through the fir-trees towards the "pigeon-house", without thinking much about what he could ask for there. He was soon checked at the edge of the wood by a little mossy wall. On the other side, between the wall and the out-houses of a manor-house there was a long narrow yard full of vehicles like the yard of an inn on a fair day. They were all kinds and shapes, small light four-seater carriages with their shafts up, charabancs, old-fashioned Bourbon coaches with moulded cornices, and even old berlins with closed windows.

Meaulnes, hidden behind the fir-trees for fear of being seen was surveying the disorder of the place, when he noticed at the other side of the yard just above the seat of a high charabanc a window in one of the out-houses which was half-open. Two iron bars like those one sees in the rear quarters of domaines whose stable shutters are kept closed, must have bolted them. But they had come open because of the weather.

"I'll go in through there," thought the student to himself. "I'll sleep in the hay and leave at dawn without having to frighten those pretty little girls."

He jumped over the wall with some difficulty because of his hurt knee, and passing from one carriage to another, and then from the seat of a charabanc on to the roof of a berlin he reached the level of the window which he pushed open silently like a door.

He found himself not in a loft full of hay but in a vast room with a low ceiling which must be a bedroom. In the semi-darkness of a Winter's evening he could make out that the table, the mantelpiece, and even the armchairs, were full of big vases, other costly items, and old weapons. At the back of the room there were some drawn curtains which seemed to conceal an alcove.

Meaulnes closed the window, not so much because of the cold, but for fear of being seen from outside. He went to lift a curtain and saw a large low bed covered with old gilded books, lutes with broken strings, and candelabras, all thrown there at random. He pushed the things aside and stretched out on the bed to rest and reflect a little on the strange adventure into which he had been thrown.

A profound silence reigned in the Domaine. Only occasionally could he hear the moaning of the great December wind.

And Meaulnes lying there began to wonder if in spite of the strange meetings, the voices of the children in the road, and the parked carriages, this wasn't simply, as he had first thought, an old-fashioned manor in the solitude of Winter.

It seemed to him soon that the wind was bearing towards him the strains of some lost music. It came like a memory full of charm and regret. He remembered how his mother when still young, used to sit at the piano in the drawing-room in the afternoon, and from behind the door which opened on to the garden he would listen silently until nightfall...

"Someone seems to be playing the piano somewhere," he thought.

But leaving the question without an answer and tormented by fatigue, he lost no time in falling asleep.

12. Wellington's Room

It was dark when he awoke. Numb with cold he turned this way and that on his bed, crumpling and rolling his black shirt underneath him. A feeble green light bathed the curtains across the alcove.

Sitting up on the bed he poked his head between the curtains. Someone had opened the window and hung two great Venetian lanterns in the recess.

But hardly had Meaulnes been able to take a peep when he heard the muffled sound of footsteps and low voices. He ducked back into the alcove and his hob-nailed shoes caught one of the bronze objects which he had pushed against the wall, and it clanged. He held his breath anxiously for a moment. The steps approached and two shadows slipped into the room.

"Don't make a noise," said one.

"It's already time he woke up," said the other.

"Have you decorated his room?"

"Yes, like everyone else's"

The wind caused the window to bang.

"But you haven't even closed the window," said the first. "The wind has already blown out one of the lanterns. We'll have to relight it."

"Bah!" said the other in a sudden fit of exasperation. "What's the good of these illuminations in the middle of the countryside? In the middle of a desert one might just as well say there's no-one to see them."

"Not no-one. Some people will arrive after dark. Down there in the road in their carriages they will be pleased to see our lights."

Meaulnes heard them strike a match. The one who had spoken last and who seemed to be the leader exclaimed in a drawling voice like a Shakespearian grave-digger,

"Put some green lanterns in Wellington's bedroom. You can put some red ones there too. You don't know any more about it than I do!"

There was a moment's silence.

"...Wellington? Was he an American? Is green an American colour? As a travelling actor you must know that."

"Huh," replied the actor, "travelled? Yes I've travelled but I haven't seen anything. What can you see in a caravan?"

Meaulnes peeped cautiously between the curtains.

The one who was directing operations was a big bare-headed man engulfed in a huge coat. In his hand he held a long pole decorated with multi-coloured lanterns, and he was sitting peacefully, one leg crossed over the other, watching his companion do the work.

As for the actor he had the most pitiful body imaginable. He was tall, emaciated, and shivering. His eyes were green and squinting, and his moustache drooped over his mouth in which some teeth were missing. He looked like a half-drowned man dripping on a flagstone. He was in his shirt-sleeves and his teeth were chattering. His words and gestures showed his utter contempt for his own person.

After a moment of reflection, at once bitter and ridiculous, he approached his partner with his arms spread out,

"Shall I tell you something? I can't understand why anyone would hire nobodies like us to serve in such a Fete!"

But ignoring this rush of feeling the big man continued to watch him as he worked, his legs crossed. He yawned and sniffed tranquilly, and then got up to leave the room, his pole over his shoulder, saying,

"Let's go. It's time for dinner."

The actor followed him, but as he passed the alcove he said with a mock bow,

"Hey you M. Sleeper. You have to get up now and dress as a marquis, even if you're only a poor wretch like me, and you have to go down to the Fete dressed in costume, since that is the wish of the little sirs and madames."

He added in a tone of unwonted humour,

"Our friend Maloyau who is attracted to the kitchens, will play the role of Harlequin, and your servant, the great Pierrot."

13. The Strange Fete

As soon as they had disappeared the student came out of his hiding-place. His feet were frozen and his joints were stiff, but he had rested and his knee seemed to be better.

"'Go down to dinner'" he thought. "I certainly shan't fail to do that! I will simply be a guest whose name everyone has forgotten. Besides I'm not an intruder here. M. Maloyau and his friend will probably be expecting me…"

Coming out from the total darkness of the alcove he could see fairly clearly in the room which was lit up by green lanterns.

The actor had decorated it. Cloaks were hung up on the coat-pegs. On the solid toilet table with its' broken marble someone had put the requisites to make a dandy out of a boy who had spent the previous night in an abandoned sheep-fold. On the mantle-piece there were matches as well as a flambeau. But the parquet floor was not polished and Meaulnes could feel sand and plaster grinding under his shoes. Again he had the impression of being in a house which had been abandoned for a long time…While going to the mantle-piece he almost stumbled against a pile of large cartons and small boxes. He reached out his arm and lit the flambeau and then raised the lids to look inside.

There were costumes for young people of long ago, frock-coats with high velvet collars, fine open waist-coats, a great many white cravats, and polished shoes from the beginning of the century. He hardly dared touch them with the tip of his finger, but after having washed, shivering, he put on one of the large cloaks over his school shirt and turned up the folded collar. He replaced his hob-nailed shoes with a pair of fine polished shoes, and prepared to go downstairs bare-headed.

He arrived at the bottom of the wooden staircase leading into a corner of the dark yard without seeing anyone. The freezing night air blew into his face and lifted the edge of his cloak.

He took a few steps, and thanks to some light from the sky he could distinguish the layout of his surroundings. The staircases were open at the bottom because the doors had been missing for a long time. No-one had replaced the window-panes, and there were black holes in the walls. And yet all the buildings had the mysterious air of a Fete. Coloured light issued from the lower rooms overlooking the land where lanterns also must have been hung. The ground was swept. The invading hedge had been trimmed back. Then, as he listened, Meaulnes thought he could hear songs and the voices of children and young girls coming from the direction of the rambling buildings where the wind shook the branches of the trees in front of the pink, green, and blue openings of the windows.

He was standing there in his big cloak like a hunter, bending slightly and listening hard, when an extraordinary little man came out from the building close by which he had thought deserted.

He was wearing a high arched hat which shone in the night like silver, a coat whose collar reached up into his hair, and open waist-coat and peg-top trousers...This elegant young man who would be about fifteen years old walked on his toes as if his feet were supported by the elastic of his trousers, yet with extraordinary rapidity. He passed by without stopping but bowing deeply and automatically to Meaulnes, and disappeared into the darkness in the direction of the central building. This was a chateau or abbey and its tower was the one which had guided the student at the beginning of the afternoon.

After a moment's hesitation our hero followed in the footsteps of the curious personage. They crossed what seemed to be a large garden and then passed through some groves, round a fish-pond surrounded by a fence, then a well, and found themselves finally on the threshold of the main building.

A heavy wooden door, arched and nailed like the door of a presbytery, was half open. The young dandy was lost inside. Meaulnes followed him, and from his first steps inside, found himself surrounded by the sound of laughter, singing, shouts and chasing...

And then another corridor intersected the one in which he stood. Meaulnes was hesitating whether he should continue along the same corridor to the end, or rather, open one of the doors behind which he could hear the voices, when he saw two little girls chasing along the far end of the corridor. He ran after them and caught up with them in his light shoes. There was the sound of the opening of doors, a glimpse of two fifteen-year-old faces which the freshness of the evening and the chase had made rosy under their big poke bonnets, and they were about to disappear in a flash of light.

For a second they spun round in fun. Their full light skirts lifted and swung out so that the lace of their amusing long pantaloons could be seen. Then, after their pirouette, they bounded together into the room and closed the door.

Meaulnes remained for a moment dazzled and staggering in the darkness. He was afraid now of being discovered. His hesitant and clumsy gait would cause him to be taken for a robber. He was about to return firmly towards the exit when again he heard further along the passage the sound of children's voices and footsteps. There were two little boys approaching and talking.

"Will it soon be dinner-time?" Meaulnes asked them with some assurance.

"Come with us," replied the older boy, "we'll take you there." And with the confidence, and need of friendship, which children have on the eve of a great Feast, they each took him by the hand. They were probably two peasant boys. Someone had dressed them in their best clothes, short trousers, and thick wool socks and galoshes, little blue velvet jerkins with caps the same colour, and white cravats tied in a bow.

"Do you know her?" asked one of the children.

The smaller child who had a round head and innocent eyes said,

"Mummy told me she has a black dress with a small collar, and that she looks like a pretty sparrow."

"Who does?" asked Meaulnes.

"The fiancée Frantz has gone to fetch..."

Before the young man could say anything more they had all three arrived at the door of a room in which a fire had been lit. Planks had been arranged on trestles to make tables, and white cloths had been spread over them. All sorts of people were dining in great ceremony.

14. The Strange Fete (cont.)

In the great room with a low ceiling a meal had been prepared like those which are served on the eve of country weddings to relatives who have traveled long distances.

The two children let go of Meaulnes' hands and rushed into an adjoining room from where he could hear the sound of children's voices and spoons on plates. Meaulnes calmly stepped over a bench and seated himself next to two old peasants. He began to eat with a voracious appetite, and only after a minute or two raised his head to look at his companions and listen to what they were saying.

In any case they spoke little. These people hardly seemed to know each other. Some of them seemed to have come from the depths of the country and others from distant towns. They were scattered along the tables, several old men with beards, and others who were completely shaved who might have been old sailors. Amongst them were similar old people, with the same tanned faces, the same lively eyes under bushy eyebrows, the same thin cravats like shoe-laces...but it was easy to see that these had never navigated further than the edge of the Canton, and if they had pitched and rolled under adversity and in the wind it was on a hard journey without peril ploughing a furrow as far as the end of a field, and returning again behind the plough...There were two old ladies with round faces wrinkled like apples under goffered bonnets...

There wasn't one among these revelers with whom Meaulnes did not feel at ease and comfortable. He explained this feeling later. He said when one has committed an unpardonable fault one dreams sometimes in the middle of one's bitterness,

"There are still people in the world who would pardon me."

And one imagines old people like grandparents, full of indulgence, who are convinced in advance that everything one does is right. Certainly these guests were such people, and the rest were adolescents and children...

Meanwhile close to Meaulnes two old ladies were gossiping.

"Even at best," said the older one in an odd shrill voice she tried vainly to soften, "the fiancés won't get here before three o'clock tomorrow."

"Oh be quiet," said the other in the most tranquil of voices, "you make me cross." This woman wore a knitted hood on her head.

"Let's see," she said comfortably, "an hour and a half by train from Bourges to Vierzon, and seven leagues in the carriage from Vierzon to here…"

The discussion continued. Meaulnes did not miss a word. Thanks to this peaceable squabble the situation became slightly clearer. Frantz de Galais was the son of the chateau and he was a student, or a sailor, or maybe he wanted to be a sailor. This wasn't clear. He had gone to Bourges to bring back a young girl and marry her. It was strange that this boy who must be very young and fantastic, could arrange everything in the Domaine as he liked. When his fiancée arrived he wanted the house to resemble a palace decorated for a Fete. And to celebrate the arrival of the young girl he had invited all these children and benevolent old people. Such were the points which emerged from the conversation between the old ladies. All the rest remained a mystery, and they returned continually to the subject of the arrival of the fiancés. One favoured the morning of the next day, the other the afternoon.

"Poor Moinelle," said the younger one calmly. "You were always foolish."

"And you Adele were always obstinate. It's four years since I last saw you and you haven't changed a bit," replied the other shrugging her shoulders, but in the gentlest tone of voice.

And they continued to argue thus good-temperedly. Meaulnes intervened hoping to learn more.

"Is Frantz's fiancée as pretty as they say?" he asked.

They looked at him, taken aback, for no-one except Frantz had seen the girl. He had met her one evening on his way back to Toulon. She was walking, desolate and alone, in the gardens of Bourges called the Marais. Her father who was a weaver had turned her out of the house. She was very pretty and Frantz had decided immediately to marry her. It was a strange story, but his father, M. de Galais and his sister Yvonne had always allowed him anything!....

Meaulnes was about to ask some more curious questions when a charming couple appeared at the door, a child of sixteen wearing a blue velvet bodice and a skirt with deep flounces, and a young personage in a coat with a high collar and elasticated pantaloons. They crossed the room dancing a step or two and others followed them. The others came in running and shouting followed by a great pale-faced Pierrot with sleeves which were too long, and a black cap, laughing with a toothless mouth. He ran in great clumsy strides as if at each step he had to jump, and he flapped his long empty sleeves. The young girls were a little afraid of him but the boys shook him by the hand and he seemed to be the cause of the joy of the children who were following him with piercing cries. He looked at Meaulnes in passing with his glassy eyes and the student believed that this was the companion of M. Maloyau the actor, although now completely shaven, who a short time ago had been hanging up the lanterns.

The meal finished and everyone rose. Rounds and farandoles* were organized in the passages. In one place a minuet was being played...Meaulnes, his head half-hidden in the collar of his cloak, like a ruff, felt to be a different person. He too was caught up in the merry-making and began to follow the great Pierrot through the passages of the Domaine. It was like being in the wings of a theatre, or in a pantomime, where everywhere the scenery is spread out. Thus he found himself for the rest of the night part of the joyous crowd in extravagant costumes. Sometimes he would find himself opening a door and entering a room where someone was showing a magic lantern and the children applauding loudly....sometimes in the corner of a room where people were dancing and he could engage some dandy in conversation and find out about the costumes which would be worn in the coming days...

A little distressed finally by all the pleasure being offered him and fearing every moment that his cloak might open and reveal his school shirt, he took refuge for a moment in the quietest and darkest area of the Domaine. He could hear the muffled sounds of the piano being played. He went into a silent room which turned out to be a

* A dance of Provence.

dining-room lit by a hanging lamp. There were decorations here also, but decorations for small children.

Some, sitting on pouffes, turned the pages of albums open on their knees. Others, crouched on the floor in front of a chair and gravely arranged a display of pictures on the seat. Others in front of the fire said nothing and did nothing, but listened from a distance in this vast Domaine to the sounds of the Fete.

A door leading from the dining-room was wide open. In the adjoining room the sound of the piano- playing could be heard. Meaulnes went and peeped in cautiously. It was a sort of parlour. A woman, or a young girl, with a great maroon cloak thrown round her shoulders, was sitting, her back towards him, playing very sweetly, airs for dancing or song. On the divan close beside her six or seven little boys and girls sat grouped as in a picture, listening as children do when it is growing late. From time to time one of them would slide to the floor and go into the dining-room, and one of the children who had been looking at pictures would go and take his place...

After the Fete where everything was charming, but feverish and mad, where he himself had so ridiculously followed the great Pierrot, here Meaulnes found himself plunged into the most peaceful happiness in the world.

Without a sound, while the young girl continued to play, he returned to sit in the dining-room and opened one of the big red books set out on the table. He began to read distractedly, but one of the little children who had been on the floor approached him, hung on to his arm and climbed on to his knee to look along with him. Then another placed himself on his other knee. It was like his dream of long ago. He felt as if he was in his own hose, married, on a beautiful evening, and the charming unknown girl playing the piano close to him was his wife...

15. The Meeting

The next morning Meaulnes was one of the first to be ready. As he had received no advice on dress he put on a simple old-fashioned black costume. It consisted of a coat which fit at the waist, a cross-over waistcoat, trousers which were so wide they hid his fine shoes, and a tall hat.

The yard was still deserted when he went down. It was the mildest day so far of that Winter. The sun shone as in the first days of April. The frost was melting and the grass shone as if it was wet with dew. In the trees several small birds sang and from time to time a cool breeze touched the face of the walker.

He did as guests do if they wake before the host. He walked in the yard of the Domaine expecting that at any moment a friendly voice would call from behind him,

"Already up, Augustin?"…

But he walked for a long time alone through the garden and the yard. In the main building nothing stirred, neither at the windows nor in the tower. Someone had already opened both of the arched wooden doors, and a ray of sunlight shone on one of the upper windows as in the early morning hours of Summer.

Meaulnes saw the inside of the property for the first time by daylight. The ruins of a wall separated the unkempt garden from the yard, where someone had recently turned over the sand and raked it. At the end of the row of outhouses where he was staying, there were some stables whose amusing disorder added to the many corners overgrown with shrubs and Virginia Creeper. Woods of fir-trees grew as far as the walls of the Domaine and concealed it from the surrounding flat countryside which stretched clear towards the East where one could see hills covered with rocks and more fir-trees.

Meaulnes leaned for a moment in the garden on a shaky wooden fence which surrounded the fish-pond. Round its' edges there was a little thin ice which was wrinkled like foam...He saw himself reflected in the water...leaning over as if against the sky in his costume of a romantic student. And he seemed to see another

Meaulnes, no longer a student who had escaped in a peasant's cart, but a charming and romantic being in some beautiful and costly book...

He was hungry so he hastened towards the main building. In the room where he had dined the evening before a peasant woman was spreading a cloth. As soon as Meaulnes was seated in front of one of the bowls set out on the cloth she poured out some coffee for him saying,

"You are the first Sir."

He did not wish to reply for fear of being recognized as a stranger. He merely asked what time the boat would leave for the morning trip which had been announced.

"Not for half an hour Sir. No-one has come down yet," was the reply.

Then he continued to wander round searching for the landing-stage. The wings of the manor house were unequal like those of a church. When he had rounded the Southern wing he suddenly came upon reeds as far as the eye could see, and bordering the path. On this side the pond water wet the base of the walls, and there were in front of several upper-floor doors, little wooden balconies which overhung the rippling waves.

Idly he wandered along the sandy footpath for a while. It was like a tow-path. He peered curiously through the dusty windows of the big doors which opened into decaying or abandoned rooms, at lumber consisting of such objects as wheelbarrows, rusty tools, and broker flower-pots, when suddenly at the other end of the buildings he heard the sound of footsteps in the sand.

There were two women, one old and bent, the other a young girl. She was blond and slender and her charming dress after the disguises of the night before appeared at first to Meaulnes as extraordinary. They paused for a moment to look at the view while Meaulnes thought to himself in an astonishment which seemed to him later as having been coarse,

"She is no doubt what is called an eccentric girl, maybe an actress who has been hired for an entertainment."

Meanwhile the two women passed close by him, and Meaulnes, immobile, watched the young girl. Often, later, when he slept after trying in despair to recall the delicate erased face, he would see passing in a dream, rows of young girls resembling this one. One would have a hat like hers, another her slightly leaning attitude, another her purity of expression, another her slender figure, another would have her blue eyes, but none of these women was ever this wonderful young girl.

Meaulnes had time to see under a mass of blond hair a face whose features were small and drawn with an almost painful delicacy. And as she passed in front of him he saw that her attire was the simplest yet most sensible of attires...

Perplexed, he was wondering if he should follow them when the girl turned slightly towards him and said to her companion,

"The boat seems to be late I think."

Meaulnes followed them. The bent and trembling old woman never ceased to chat gaily and to laugh, and the girl replied gently. And when they arrived at the jetty she had the same innocent and grave expression on her face which seemed to ask,

"Who are you? What are you doing here? And yet it seems to me that I recognize you."

Other guests were now scattered under the trees waiting, and three pleasure boats drew in ready to receive the strollers. One by one as the two ladies who seemed to be the chatelaine and her daughter passed by, the boys took off their hats and bowed low and the girls inclined their heads. Strange morning! Strange pleasure party! It was cold in spite of the Winter sun and the women wrapped the feather boas which were the fashion round their necks...

The old lady remained behind on the bank and without thinking Meaulnes found himself in the same boat with the young chatelaine. As he leaned on the bridge holding his hat in his hand because of the wind he could watch the young girl at his ease, sitting in the shade. She too was looking back at him. She would respond to her companions with a smile and then turn her eyes sweetly towards him, biting her lip a little.

A great silence reigned in the neighbouring barges. The boat slid along with only the sound of the machine and the lapping water. It might have been the height of Summer. They were to disembark, it seemed, in the beautiful garden of a neighbouring house. The young girl would walk there under a parasol. They would hear the turtle-doves cooing until evening. But suddenly a gust of wind reminded the guests of this strange Fete, that this was December.

They alighted in front of a fir-tree wood. On the landing-stage the passengers paused for a moment, holding on to each other until one of the boatmen had opened the padlock of the barrier...With what emotion Meaulnes remembered this moment later when by the lake-side he had the face of the young girl so close to his own! He had looked at the purity of her profile with all his eyes until they were almost filling with tears. And he remembered seeing like a delicate secret she had confided to him a trace of powder on her cheek...

On landing everything seemed as in a dream. While the children ran about with cries of joy and other groups dispersed towards the woods, Meaulnes followed along a path where ten paces in front of him the young girl walked. Without thinking he found himself close to her.

"You are beautiful," he said simply.

But she hastened her step and without replying turned on to another path. Other walkers ran and played along the avenues, each wandering as he liked, led only by his fancy. The young man reproached himself for what he felt to be his blunder, his coarseness, his foolishness. He walked along at random persuaded that he would not see the gracious creature again when he suddenly caught sight of her coming in his direction. She would have to pass close by him on the narrow path. She opened the folds of her heavy cloak with bare hands. She wore thin black shoes. The hairs of her head were so fine that when they were bent by the breeze one feared that they might break.

This time the young man bowed and said in a low voice,

"Will you forgive me?"

"I forgive you," she said gravely, "but I must go back to the children since they are in charge today. Goodbye."

Augustin begged her to remain for a moment. He spoke awkwardly, but in so agitated a tone and in so much confusion that she walked more slowly to listen to him.

"I don't even know who you are," she said at last.

She pronounced each word with even stress and tone, but spoke the last word more gently...Then   she turned her impassive face away, biting her lip a little, her blue eyes staring into the distance.

"I do not even know your name," replied Meaulnes.

They were walking now along an open path and could see some of the guests in the distance collecting round a house which was isolated in the surrounding countryside.

"That is Frantz's house," said the girl. "I will have to leave you..." She hesitated, and looked at him for a moment smiling.

"My name?" she said. "I am Mademoiselle Yvonne de Galais..." And she escaped.

"Frantz's house" was inhabited then. But Meaulnes found it occupied to the attics by the crowd of guests. He hardly had time even to examine the place at leisure. They had a hurried cold breakfast which they had brought in the boats. It was unsuitable for the season but probably the children had planned it this way. Then they returned. Meaulnes approached Mlle de Galais as soon as he saw her coming out, replying to what she had recently told him.

"The name I gave you was more beautiful," he said.

"Oh? And what name was that?" she asked with the same gravity. But he was afraid of having committed a blunder and did not reply.

"My own name is Augustin Meaulnes," he said, "and I am a student."

"Oh, you study?" she said, and they spoke for a moment more. They spoke slowly, with happiness, with friendship. Then the attitude of the young girl changed. It was less distant and less grave but at the same time more uneasy. Close at his side she trembled like a swallow which has alighted on the ground for a moment and already quivers in its' desire to resume its' flight.

"What would be the point?" she asked gently to all Meaulnes' suggestions. But when finally he dared ask permission to return one day to this beautiful house she replied simply,

"I'll wait for you."

They were in view now of the place of embarkation. She stopped suddenly and said pensively,

"We are two children. We have committed a folly. We shouldn't get into the same boat this time. Adieu. Don't follow me."

Meaulnes remained motionless for a moment watching her depart. Then he began to walk again. And the young girl in the distance, as she was about to be lost in the crowd of guests, paused and turned towards him and looked at him for a long moment. Was it a last signal of adieu? Was it to forbid him to accompany her? Or was there perhaps something else she wished to say to him?....

As soon as they returned to the Domaine there was a pony race in the big sloping field behind the farm. This was the last part of the Fete. According to the forecasts the fiancés were supposed to arrive in time for it, and Frantz was supposed to be in charge of the arrangements.

They had to begin without him however. The boys were dressed as jockeys, and the girls as horse-women. The former brought the beribboned frisky ponies, and the latter the old docile horses amidst shouts of childish laughter, bets, and long peals of bells. They seemed to have been transported on the grass and newly mown turf to some miniature race-course.

Meaulnes recognized Daniel and the little girls with the feathered hats whom he had seen the evening before on the path in the woods...The rest of the spectacle escaped him, so anxious was he to spy in the crowd the graceful hat of roses and the big chestnut – brown cloak. But Mlle de Galais did not appear. He searched for her until shouts and peals of bells announced the end of the races. A little girl on an old white mare had won. She passed by triumphant on her mount, and the plumes of her hat floated in the wind.

Then suddenly everything went quiet. The games were over and Frantz had not returned. There was some hesitation and people consulted each other awkwardly. Finally in groups they returned to their apartments to wait anxiously in the silence for the return of the fiancés.

16. Frantz de Galais

The race had finished too early. It was half-past four and still light when Meaulnes reached his room, his head full of the events of his extraordinary day. He sat idly in front of the table waiting for dinner and the party which would follow.

The great wind of the previous evening blew again. It could be heard groaning like a mountain stream or passing with the sustained whistle of a waterfall. The damper in the grate shook from time to time.

For the first time Meaulnes felt the slight pain of regret which seizes one at the end of a few days of great happiness. He thought for a moment of lighting the fire, but he tried in vain to move the rusty damper from the chimney. The he began to walk about the room. He hung his fine clothes on the coat pegs and arranged the upset chairs along the walls as if he were preparing everything for a long stay.

Thinking that he should make ready to leave he folded his shirt and other student's clothes carefully over the back of a chair. He placed his hob-nailed shoes still full of earth under the chair.

Then he sat down again, more at peace, and looked around at his room which he had put in order.

From time to time a drop of water would streak the window-pane which looked down over the yard where the carriages stood, and across to the wood of fir-trees.

Tranquil since he had arranged his room, the boy felt perfectly happy. He was there, mysterious, a stranger, in the middle of an unknown world, in the room he had chosen. What he had experienced had surprised all his expectations. And he was content now with the joy of remembering the face of the young girl in the wind turning towards him...

During this reverie night had fallen without it occurring to him to light his candles. A gust of wind made the door of the adjoining room, which communicated with his own, bang. Meaulnes was going to close it when he saw a light in the room. The candle on the table must have been lit. He advanced towards the opening of the door.

Someone had entered by the window no doubt and was walking back and forth silently. As far as he could see it was a very young man. Bare-headed and wearing a travelling-cape round his shoulders he walked without pausing like someone maddened by an unsupportable anguish. The wind through the window which he had left wide open made his cape flap, and every time he passed close to the light the gilt buttons on his fine frock coat gleamed.

He whistled something between his teeth. It was some sort of sailors' song like those sailors and girls sang in the cabarets in the ports to cheer their hearts...

For a moment in the middle of his agitated walk he stopped and leaned on the table, searching in a box and taking out several sheets of paper...Meaulnes saw in the light of the candle a very fine profile, very aquiline, without a moustache, under an abundance of hair which was parted at one side. He had stopped whistling. Very pale and his lips parted he seemed to be out of breath like someone who has received a violent blow on the heart.

Meaulnes hesitated whether to retire discreetly, or advance and put his hand gently on his shoulder, like a comrade, and speak to him. But the other raised his head and saw him. He considered him for a moment and then without astonishment approached him, steadying his voice,

"Monsieur, I don't know you but I'm happy to see you. Since you are here it is to you that I will explain things...

You see..."

He seemed to be completely wretched. When he said 'you see' he took hold of Meaulnes by the lapels of his jacket to fix his attention. Then he turned his head towards the window to reflect what he was going to say, and closed his eyes tightly. Meaulnes realized he was trying not to cry.

He repressed the childish emotion with an effort, and then still gazing fixedly at the window, he spoke in an altered voice,

"Well, you see, it's over. The party is over. You can go down and tell them that. I have come home alone. My fiancée won't be coming. Because of some scruple, some fear, some loss of faith...besides Monsieur...I will explain to you...."

But he could not continue. His whole face crumpled. He explained nothing. Turning away suddenly he went into the dark part of the room to open and close drawers full of clothes and books.

"I'm going to get ready to leave," he said, "so that no-one upsets me."

He placed various objects on the table, toilet necessities, a pistol...

And Meaulnes, full of confusion, left without daring to say a word to him or shake hands.

Below already people seemed to have sensed something. Almost all the little girls had changed their clothes. In the main building dinner had commenced, but hastily and in disorder as at the moment of departure. There was continual coming and going between the dining-room and the other rooms and the stables. Those who had finished were forming groups and making their farewells.

"What's happening?" Meaulnes asked one country boy who was hurrying to complete his meal with his felt hat on his head and his napkin tucked into his waistcoat.

"We're leaving," he replied. "It was decided suddenly. At five o'clock all of us guests found ourselves alone. We had waited till the last moment. The fiancés could not be coming. Then someone said, 'should we leave?' and everyone got ready to go."

Meaulnes did not reply. It did not matter to him now. Hadn't he come to the end of his adventure? Hadn't he obtained for the moment all that he desired?

He had not even had time yet to remember at leisure the whole of the sweet conversation of the morning. Just now it was merely a question of departure. And soon he would return....without trickery this time.

"If you want to come with us," went on the other who was a boy his own age, "hurry up and get ready. We are going to hitch up the horses in a minute."

He ran off at a gallop leaving his meal which he had begun and neglecting to tell the guests what he knew. The park, the garden, the yard were plunged in darkness. This evening there were no lanterns at the windows. But because, after all, this last dinner resembled the last meal of the eve of a marriage, the least well-behaved of the guests who had perhaps been drinking, began to sing. As he left,

Meaulnes could hear their cabaret songs in the park in which for the last two days had witnessed such grace and marvels. And this was the beginning of disarray and devastation. He passed close by the fish-pond in which only that morning he had he had looked at himself. How changed everything was already... with this song whose chorus he caught in snatches:

"From where then are you returning little libertine?
Your bonnet is torn, your hair awry?"

And the refrain:
My shoes are red...
Goodbye my lovers....
My shoes are red....
Goodbye for ever!

As he arrived at the foot of the staircase to his isolated room, someone was coming down them and bumped against him in the darkness, and said to him,

"Goodbye Monsieur!"

And wrapping himself in his cape as if he was very cold, he disappeared. It was Frantz de Galais.

The candle which Frantz had left in his room was still burning. Nothing had been disturbed. There was only, written on a piece of writing paper and placed prominently, these words:

"My fiancée has disappeared, telling me that she cannot be my wife; that she is a dress-maker and not a princess. I don't know what will happen. I'm leaving. I no longer want to live. I hope that Yvonne will forgive me if I do not say goodbye, but she will not be able to do anything for me..."

That was the end of the candle whose flame was flickering, dimmed a second and then went out. Meaulnes returned to his own room and closed the door. In spite of the darkness, he could distinguish all the things he had arranged in daylight, in great happiness a few hours earlier. Piece by piece he retrieved faithfully all his old shabby clothes from his old-fashioned shoes to his heavy buckled leather belt. He undressed and dressed again quickly but distractedly, placing his borrowed clothes on a chair but forgetting his waist-coat......

Beneath the windows in the carriage yard a household-removal had begun. Someone pulled, someone shouted, someone pushed; each wishing to extricate his vehicle from the jumbled confusion in which it was trapped. From time to time a man would climb on to the driving-seat of a carriage or to the canopy of a large wagon and turn his lantern round. Light would strike the window: for a moment around Meaulnes the now familiar room, where everything had been for him so friendly, so exciting, was revived...And it was thus that he left, carefully closing the door, that mysterious place which he would probably never see again.

17. The Strange Fete (conclusion)

Already, in the darkness, a line of carriages was rolling slowly towards the gate into the wood. At the head, a man dressed in a goat-skin, a lantern in his hand, led the horse of the first carriage by the bridle.

Meaulnes made haste to find someone who would take him. He was in a hurry to leave. In his heart he feared being left suddenly alone in the Domaine and his fraud discovered.

When he arrived in front of the main building the drivers were balancing the weight of the occupants of the last carriages. They were assisting the travelers to adjust their seating, and the young girls wrapped in shawls climbed up awkwardly as the covers fell to their feet, and he could see the anxious faces of those who bent their heads near the lanterns.

In one of the drivers Meaulnes recognized the young peasant who a short while earlier had offered to take him.

"Can I come up?" he called to him.

"Where are you going boy?" replied the other who no longer recognized him.

"In the direction of Sainte-Agathe."

"Then you'll have to go with Maritain."

And the big student searched among the remaining travelers for the unknown Maritain. He was pointed out to him among some drinkers who were singing in the kitchen.

"He's a bit of a reveler," someone said. "He'll still be there at three o'clock in the morning."

Meaulnes thought for a moment of the young girl in the Domaine and her feverish distress as she listened to these drunken peasants singing well into the middle of the night. In which room was she? Where was her window among these mysterious buildings? But nothing served to detain the student. He had to go. Once back in Sainte-Agathe everything would be clearer. He would cease to be a student who had run away. He would be able to dream again of the young chatelaine.

One by one the carriages left. The wheels creaked in the sand of the drive, and in the night they could be seen turning and disappearing, full of muffled women and children in shawls who were already asleep. One more big carriage, a trap in which the women sat shoulder to shoulder passed by leaving Meaulnes speechless on the threshold of the Domaine. He did not have to remain there long before an old berlin arrived, driven by a peasant in a smock.

"You can come up," he replied to Meaulnes' request. "We are going in that direction".

Painfully Meaulnes opened the door of the old wagon in which the windows trembled and the hinges squeaked. On a bench in the corner of the carriage two small children, a boy and a girl, were asleep. They awoke to the noise and the cold, stretched, looked round vaguely, then shivered and snuggled back into their corner and slept again.

The old carriage was already leaving. Meaulnes closed the door again softly and sat carefully in the other corner; then hungrily he tried to distinguish through the glass the places he was leaving and the route by which he had come. He guessed in spite of the darkness that the carriage was crossing the yard and the garden, passing in front of the staircase to her room, passing through the gate and out of the Domaine to enter the woods. Vanishing across the window-pane he could make out vaguely the trunks of the old fir-trees.

"Perhaps we will meet Frantz de Galais," thought Meaulnes with a beating heart.

Abruptly in the narrow path the carriage swerved to avoid an obstacle. It was, as far as he could see in the dark amongst their massive forms, a stationary vehicle in the middle of the path, and it must have been standing there close to the Fete throughout those recent days.

The obstacle overcome, the horses set off at a trot. Meaulnes began to tire of looking through the window and trying to see anything in the darkness. Suddenly there was a flash followed by a shot. The horses rushed forward at a gallop, and Meaulnes did not know whether the coachman in the smock was trying to hold them back or on the contrary was urging them to flee. He wanted to open the door. As the handle was on the outside he tried vainly to open the window. He shook it. The children woke in fear and clung to each other silently. And as he shook the window, his face glued to the pane, he saw, thanks to a bend in the road, a white form running, frantic and haggard. It was the big Pierrot of the Fete, the actor, still in his fancy dress and carrying in his arms close to his chest, a human body. Then he disappeared.

In the carriage which fled at a gallop through the night the two children slept again. There was no-one with whom he could talk about the mysterious events of those two days. Having gone over in his mind all that he had seen and heard, weary with fatigue and his heart heavy, the young man also abandoned himself to sleep like a sad child…..

It was not yet dawn when the carriage stopped in the road. Meaulnes was awakened by someone knocking at the window. The driver opened the door with difficulty and cried, as the cold night air froze the student to the bones,

"You'll have to get down here. It's sunrise. We are approaching the turning now. You are quite close to Sainte-Agathe."

Meaulnes obeyed, searching vaguely with an unconscious gesture for his cap which had rolled under the feet of the sleeping children in the darkest corner of the carriage. Then he stepped down.

"Well. Goodbye," said the man climbing back to his seat. "You have no more than six kilometers to go. See, the boundary mark is there by the road."

Meaulnes who had not yet awoken fully from his sleep walked, bent over, towards the boundary mark and sat down, his arms crossed and his head forward as if to go to sleep again.

"Hey! No!" shouted the driver, "You mustn't sleep there. It's too cold. Come on, stand up, walk a bit…"

Wobbling like a drunk man, the big boy, his hands in his pockets, his shoulders hunched, walked away slowly along the road to Sainte-Agathe, while the last remnant of the mysterious Fete, the old berlin, left the gravel road and disappeared, jolting in silence along the grassy path. Only the driver's hat could be seen dancing along above the fence…..

PART II

1. The Great Game

The strong wind and the cold, the rain and the snow, made it impossible for Meaulnes and myself to conduct long researches or speak again of the lost country before the end of Winter. We could not begin anything serious during the short days of February or the squally Thursdays which ended regularly towards five o'clock in dismal icy rain.

Nothing reminded us of Meaulnes' adventure except for the strange fact that since the afternoon of his return we no longer had any friends. At recreation the same games were organised as before but Jasmin no longer spoke to Meaulnes. In the evenings as soon as the classroom was swept, the yard emptied just as in the days when I was alone, and I would see my companion wander from the garden to the shed, and from the yard to the dining-room.

Thursday mornings, each of us, seated at desks in one of the two classrooms would read Rousseau and Paul-Louis Courier whose books we had unearthed in the cupboards from among English grammars and neatly copied music exercise-books. In the afternoons some visitor would cause us to abandon the house sometimes and return to the school..Sometimes we would listen to groups of senior students who would pause as if by chance in front of the main gate and strike it while playing incomprehensible military games and then go away…This melancholy life continued until the end of February. I began to think Meaulnes had forgotten everything, when an adventure more strange than the others proved to me that I was mistaken and that a violent crisis was developing beneath the dreary surface of that wintry existence.

It was late on Thursday evening when the first news of the strange Domaine, the first wave of the adventure of which we did not speak, reached us. It was evening time. My grand-parents had gone. There remained with us only Millie and my father who knew nothing of the silent quarrel, because of which the entire class was divided into two factions.

At eight o'clock Millie, who had opened the door to throw out crumbs, exclaimed,

"Oh!" in such a loud voice that we went to see. On the door-step there was a layer of snow...As it was very dark I advanced a few steps into the yard to see if the layer was deep. I felt light flakes fall on my body and settle immediately. As a result I returned inside again quickly, and Millie closed the door again with a shiver.

At nine o'clock we made ready to climb upstairs to bed. My mother had the lamp already in her hand when we heard quite clearly two heavy blows strike the gate at the other end of the yard with full force. She replaced the lamp on the table and we remained standing, alert and listening.

It was not possible to go and see what was happening. Before we had crossed even a fraction of the yard the lamp would have gone out, and my father had started to say, "I expect it was...", when just under the dining-room window which faced, as I have said, the road to the station, there was a whistle, strident and prolonged, which could have been heard as far as the church road. And immediately, outside the window, hardly muffled by the panes which were being pushed by people who had climbed on to the window-sill, there were cries of,

"Come on! Come on!"

At the other end of the building similar cries replied. These people must have come across old M. Martin's field. They would have had to climb on to the low wall which separated the field from the yard.

Then the shouts of eight or ten unknown persons in disguised voices, "Come on!" echoed successively on the roof of the store-room which they must have reached by climbing the pile of wood leaning against its' outside wall, then the little wall which ran between the store and the gate, and whose rounded top provided a convenient perch for mounting a horse, then the grilled wall along the route to the station which could easily be climbed, and finally, behind, in the garden, a group of late-comers arrived making the same hullaballoo, and crying now,

"On board!"

And we heard the echo of their cries reverberate in the empty classrooms whose windows they had opened.

We knew so well, Meaulnes and I, all the routes and passages of the great house, that we could see clearly, as if on a plan, all the points which the unknown people were attacking.

To tell the truth it was only in the first moment that we were afraid. The whistle made all four of us think of gypsies or travelling-players. In fact in the square behind the church there had been for about a fortnight a large ill-looking fellow and a young boy with his head wrapped in a bandage. There were also at the wheel-wright's and the blacksmith's some labourers who were not of the district.

But as soon as we heard the assailants shouting we were persuaded that these were those people along with probably some young people from the town. There were even some boys whose shrill voices we could recognize in the troop which threw themselves into the assault on our home like sailors boarding a ship. My father cried,

"Or for instance..." and asked Millie in a low voice,

"What is the meaning of all this?"

Then suddenly the voices at the gate and from the grilled wall, then those at the window, stopped. There were two whistles from behind the window. The cries of those who had climbed on to the window-sill, like those of the assailants in the garden, diminished gradually and then ceased. Along the dining-room wall we heard the sounds of the gang retreating quickly, their footsteps deadened in the snow.

Evidently someone had disturbed them. At this hour when everything was quiet they had expected to lead their assault on this isolated house on the outskirts of the town in peace, but here was someone upsetting their plan of campaign.

"M. Seurel! M. Seurel!"

It was M. Pasquier, the butcher. The fat little man scraped his clogs on the step, shook out his short smock which was sprinkled with snow, and entered. He had the cunning and alarming manner of one who has surprised the secret of a mysterious affair.

"I was in my yard which looks out on to the Quatre-Routes square. I was just going to close the goats' shed, when suddenly, standing in the snow, what do I see? Two big boys who seemed to be standing on guard or watching over something. They were near the cross. I take two steps, and hop! Off they go at full gallop in your direction. I didn't hesitate. I took my lantern and said, "I'll go and see M. Seurel....."And there he was to tell his story, and was about to tell it all over again.

"I was in my yard behind my house..." At this stage he was offered a liqueur which he accepted, and was asked to give details which he was unable to furnish.

He did not see anything on arriving at the house. The gangs who had been alerted by the two sentinels whom he had disturbed had disappeared. As for saying who these raiders would be.......

"They could have been travelling players," he suggested. "For about a month they have been in the square waiting for good weather to put on their play. They could have organized some sort of attack."

All this hardly got us anywhere, and we were standing very perplexed while the man sipped his liqueur and repeated his story again, when Meaulnes who had listened so far very attentively, took the butcher's lantern and said,

"We must go and see!"

He opened the door and we followed him, M. Seurel, M. Pasquier, and myself.

Millie, already reassured since the assailants had left, and like all orderly meticulous people, had a very incurious nature, declared,

"Go and see if you want. But close the door and lock it. I'm going to bed. I'll leave the lamp lit."

2. We Fall into an Ambush

We emerged into snow and profound silence. Meaulnes walked in front, throwing out from his grilled lantern a fan-shaped light. Hardly had we passed through the main gate when from behind the municipal weighing-machine, which stood against the wall of our yard, two cloaked figures shot out like a couple of surprised pigeons. Possibly in mockery, or possibly out of pleasure in the strange game they were playing, or nervous excitement and fear of being caught, they spoke two or three words cut short by laughter as they ran.

Meaulnes let the lantern fall into the snow and shouted to me, "Follow me Francois!..."

And leaving behind the two older men who were not able to do likewise, we threw ourselves into pursuit of the two shadows which after a moment by-passed the end of the town and took the Vieille-Planche road which led straight to the church. They ran evenly without too much haste and we had no difficulty in keeping up with them. They crossed the church road where everything was silent and asleep, and turned in behind the cemetery into a maze of small streets and cul-de-sacs.

This was the district of journalists and weavers and dress-makers which was called the Petits-Coins. We did not know it well and had never come there by night. The place was deserted during the day. The journalists were absent and the weavers indoors. And in the silence of that night it seemed even more abandoned. Even more were asleep than in other areas of the town. There was therefore no chance of anyone appearing and giving us any assistance.

I knew only one route between these small houses set at random like cardboard boxes. It was that which led to the dress-maker's, called "La Muette". One went first down a fairly steep slope which was flagged in places, and then after taking two or three turns between weavers' yards and empty stables one arrived at a dead-end. The way was blocked by the yard of a farm which had long since been abandoned. At "La Muette's" or the "Dumb Lady's" establishment, since she engaged my mother in conversation with movements of the fingers, the silence was broken only by the feeble cries of a mute, I would look through the window at the great wall of the farm which was the last house on that side of the town. The gate was always closed and the yard dry, without straw, and no-one ever went there any more..........

It was this same road which the two strangers took. At each turning we feared to lose them, but to my surprise each time we rounded a corner into a street before they had left it. I say "to my surprise" because all the streets were short and it would not have been possible unless they had slackened pace every time we were lost from view.

At last they turned into the road leading to "La Muette's" and I called to Meaulnes,

"We'll catch them. It's a dead-end!"

To tell the truth it was they who were leading us. They had taken us where they wanted us to go. When they reached the wall they turned towards us resolutely and one of them gave the whistle we had already heard twice that evening.

Immediately a dozen boys emerged from the abandoned farmyard where they seem to have been posted to wait for us. They were wrapped in cloaks and their faces buried in scarves...

Who it was we already knew but had been determined not to say anything to M. Seurel so that our affairs should not be seen. They were Delouche, Denis, Giraudat, and all the others. We had recognized in their attack both their style and their voices. But one point remained disturbing and it seemed almost to frighten Meaulnes. There was someone whom we did not know and who seemed to be their chief...

He did not touch Meaulnes. He watched his soldiers manoevering. They had much to do struggling in the snow and grappling with the big panting boy. The two who were occupied with me had immobilised me with difficulty for I fought like a devil. I was on the ground, my knees bent, and squatting on my heels. One held my arms behind my back and I watched the scene with intense curiosity mixed with fear.

Meaulnes had thrown off four of the school-boys by turning violently to loosen their hold on his shirt and tossing them with all his strength into the snow...Standing erect the unknown figure followed the battle with calm interest, saying from time to time in a steady voice,

"Come along...have courage...bring him here...go on boys...."

It was clearly he who commanded them...from where had he come? And how had he trained them to fight? This remained a mystery to us. Like the others his face was wrapped in a scarf, but when Meaulnes had thrown off his adversaries and advanced towards him menacingly, the movement he made to see the situation more clearly revealed a portion of white linen which was wrapped round his head like a bandage.

It was at that moment that I shouted to Meaulnes,

"See behind you! There's another one."

He hardly had time to react before from behind the wall to which his back had been turned a great devil leapt and skillfully passed his scarf round my friend's neck and pulled him over from behind. Immediately the former adversaries whom Meaulnes had thrust into the snow returned to the charge to immobilise his arms and legs. They tied his arms with a cord and his legs with a scarf, and the young personage with a bandaged head felt in his pockets...The last arrival, the man with the lasso, had lit a small candle which he protected with his hand, and each time he found another paper the leader went close to the candle to see what it contained. He unfolded at last a sort of map covered with inscriptions, the one on which Meaulnes had worked since his return, and cried with joy:

"This time we have it. Here is the plan! Here is the guide! We are going to see if this gentleman has been where I think..."

His acolyte put out the candle. Each of the boys picked up his cap and his belt. And they all departed as silently as they had come, leaving me free to run and untie my companion.

"He won't get very far with that plan," said Meaulnes as he stood up.

And we left slowly as he was limping a little. On the church road we met M. Seurel and old Pasquier.

"Didn't you see anything?" they asked..."We saw nothing!"

Thanks to the darkness of the night they had not seen anything. The butcher left us and M. Seurel returned quickly to go to bed. But we two, in our room above, by the light which Millie had left for us, sat for a long time patching up our clothes where they had come unstitched, and discussing in low voices what had happened to us, just like companions-at-arms on the evening after a lost battle...

3. The Travelling Actor at School

Wakening next morning was painful. At eight o'clock when M. Seurel went to give the signal to enter, we arrived breathless to take our places in the lines. As we were late we slid in anywhere, though normally big Meaulnes was the first in the long line of students standing shoulder to shoulder and had the job of being in charge of the exercise-books, text-books and pen-holders while M. Seurel examined them.

I was surprised by the silent eagerness with which we were given places towards the middle of the line, and while M. Seurel delayed big Meaulnes' entry into the yard for a few seconds for the inspection, I leaned my head forward curiously to right and left to observe the faces of our enemies of the evening before.

The first one I saw was he of whom I had not ceased to think, but the last I could have expected to see in this place. He was in Meaulnes' usual place, the first of all. One foot was on the stone step and one shoulder and the corner of the bag he carried on his back leaned against the frame of the door. His delicate pale face, a little touched with pink, was turned towards us with a sort of amused and scornful curiosity. His head and half of his face were bandaged in white linen. I recognized the chief of the band, the young travelling-actor, who had robbed us the night before.

But already we were entering the classroom and taking our places. The new pupil sat near the pillar to the left of the long bench on which Meaulnes occupied the first place at the other end. Giraudat, Delouche, and three others had squeezed up close together to give him space, as if by previous arrangement...

Often in Winter chance pupils would stay with us thus. They might be sailors held up by the frozen canals, or apprentices, or travellers who were snow-bound. They stayed in the class for a couple of days, or a month, rarely more...Objects of curiosity in the first hour, they were also neglected, and soon disappeared in the crowd of regular pupils.

But this one would not let himself be forgotten like that. I remember still that singular being and all the strange treasures he carried in the satchel on his back. First there was a pen with a little view set into it which he took out to write his dictation. When one closed one eye to look through the eye-hole in the handle, one could see, indistinct and in close-up, the Basilica of Lourdes or some such monument. He chose someone to look first and everyone immediately passed it from hand to hand. Then there was the Chinese pencil-box in which there was a compass and other interesting instruments, and this was passed along the bench to the left, silently and slyly, from hand to hand under the exercise-books so that M. Seurel could not see anything.

Brand new books were also passed along whose titles I would read covetously on the covers of some of the few books in our library: "Blackbirds of La Teppe", "Seagulls of La Roche", "My Friend Benoist"...Some leafed through these volumes on their knees with one hand and wrote their dictation with the other. We did not know where they had come from, stolen perhaps. Others turned the compasses in the bottom of their desks. Others again, while M. Seurel turned his back and continued the dictation while walking from the desk to the window, closed one eye to see the spotted and blue-green view of Notre-Dame of Paris. And the strange pupil, his pen in his hand, his delicate profile against the grey of the pillar, winked his eye, enjoying the furtive game which he had set in motion round him.

Meanwhile gradually the whole class was becoming disturbed. The objects which were being passed along systematically reached, one after the other, the hands of Meaulnes, who put them down carelessly beside him without looking at them. He soon had a pile like the mathematical and colourful array at the feet of the woman who represents science in allegorical pictures. Inevitably M. Seurel was going to discover this strange collection and realize the game. He might think, in addition, into enquiring into the events of the night. The presence of the travelling-actor would make his job easy...

80

Soon, indeed, he stopped, surprised, in front of big Meaulnes.

"Whose is all this?" he asked, pointing to "all this" with the back of his book closed over his index-finger.

"I don't know anything about it," said Meaulnes gruffly without raising his head.

But the unknown student intervened:

"It's mine," he said.

And he added the large and extravagant gesture of a young aristocrat which the elderly school-teacher did not know how to resist.

"Well I place them at your disposal Monsieur, if you care to see them."

In a few seconds without a sound, in order not to disturb the new state of things which had been established, the whole class gathered curiously round the master, who bent over the treasure, his half-bald curly head close to the pale young personage who with an air of tranquil triumph gave the necessary explanations. Meanwhile, silent at his bench and completely abandoned, big Meaulnes had opened his rough book, wrinkling his brow, and applied himself to a different problem.

Recess surprised us in these preoccupations. The dictation was not finished and disorder reigned in the classroom. To tell the truth it had been recreation all morning.

At half-past ten when the dark muddy yard was invaded by the students it was soon evident that a new leader controlled the games.

Of all the new amusements the travelling-actor introduced to us that morning I remember only the most bloody. It was a kind of tournament where the horses were the bigger students, and the younger ones climbed on to their shoulders. They were divided into two teams which started from the two ends of the play-ground. They bore down on each other trying to bring their adversaries to the ground. The clash was violent with the knights using their scarves as lassoes and their arms stretched like spears trying to unseat their opponents. There were some who avoided the collision, but lost their balance and pitched into the mud, the knight rolling under his mount. There were boys who were half-unseated but were retrieved by their legs by their horses and went anew fiercely into battle.

Mounted on big Delage who had very long limbs, red hair, and sticking-out ears, the thin knight with the bandaged head incited the two rival groups, and directed his mount scornfully with shouts of laughter.

Augustin, standing on the doorstep of the classroom, at first watched maliciously as the game was being organized. And I was beside him, undecided.

"He's a smart fellow," he said between his teeth. "Coming here this morning was the only way of not being suspected. M. Seurel let himself be taken in!"

He remained there for some time, his shaved head in the wind, grumbling about the actor who was going to take charge of all these boys of whom he had recently been the captain. And peaceable child that I was I could not help agreeing.

Everywhere, in every corner, in the absence of the master, the battle continued. The smaller boys ended up climbing on each other. They ran and fell head over heels, even before being knocked down by an adversary...Soon the only people remaining standing in the yard was a fierce and turbulent group in the middle of which the white bandage of the new leader could be seen bobbing every few moments.

Then Meaulnes could bear it no longer. He lowered his head, and put his hands on his hips crying,

"Come on Francois!"

Surprised by this sudden decision I nevertheless jumped without hesitation on to his shoulders and in a second we were in the thick of the fight while most of the frenzied combatants fled shouting,

"Here's Meaulnes! Here comes big Meaulnes!"

In the middle of those who remained he began to spin round saying to me, "Stretch out your arms. Grab them as I did last night."

And I, intoxicated by the battle, certain of triumph, clutched at the younger boys as they passed. They struggled and rocked for a moment on the shoulders of the big boys and fell into the mud, while there remained only the newcomer mounted on Delage, but he did not want to engage in battle with Augustin. Delage jerked his back straight and forced the white knight to descend.

With one hand on the shoulder of his mount, as a captain holds the bit of his horse, the boy stood on the ground looking at big Meaulnes with some emotion and immense admiration.

"It's only the beginning!" he said.

But at that moment the bell rang dispersing the students who had gathered round us expecting an interesting scene. And Meaulnes, deprived of throwing his enemy to the ground, turned his back sourly.

"It will wait for another time!"

Until mid-day the class continued in the way it does when holidays are approaching, amusements and conversation intervening in which the actor-student was the centre.

He explained how since they were immobilized by the cold, in the square, and could not plan nightly performances to which no-one would come, they had decided that he should come to school to keep him occupied during the day, while his companion looked after the birds (oiseaux des Iles), and the performing goat. Then he talked about travels in the neighbouring countryside and how a shower fell on the poor zinc roof of their caravan and they had had to climb down to push the wheels. The less romantic profited by the occasion to warm themselves in front of the stove. But soon curiosity overcame them also and they joined the talkative group to listen, while keeping a hand on top of the stove to keep their place.

"And what do you live on?" asked M. Seurel, who was following it all with a rather childish curiosity for a school-master, and asking a lot of questions.

The boy hesitated for a moment, as if he had never worried about such a detail.

"Why," he said, "on what we earned last Autumn I think. Ganache keeps the accounts."

No-one asked who Ganache was. But I thought of the great devil who the night before had attacked Meaulnes treacherously from behind and had knocked him down...

4.   In which it is a Question of the Mysterious Domaine

The afternoon brought the same pleasures, and all over the school-yard the same disorder and the same cold. The actor had brought more precious objects, shells, games, songs, and even a little monkey which scratched quietly inside his satchel...M. Seurel paused continually to see what the artful boy was going to bring out of his bag next...Four o'clock came and Meaulnes was the only one who had finished his problems.

We emerged from the classroom without haste. There was no longer, it seemed, that sharp division between class-time and recreation which made school-life simple and regulated like the succession of night and day. We forgot even at ten to four to tell M Seurel, as we usually did, which pupils would sweep the classroom. We never failed to do this normally because it was a way of announcing and hastening the departure into the yard.

Chance ordained that that day it was the turn of big Meaulnes, and that morning I had warned the actor while talking to him that new pupils were always given the job of being second sweeper on the day of their arrival.

Meaulnes returned to the classroom as soon as he had looked for bread of his choice. As for the actor, he took his time and arrived at last, running, as if night was already beginning to fall....

"You stay in the classroom," my companion had told me, "and while I hold him, you get back the plan he stole from me."

I sat therefore at a little table, near the window reading by the light of the day, and I saw them both moving the school benches in silence – big Meaulnes taciturn and his countenance closed, his black shirt buttoned with three buttons behind and belted;   the other delicate, nervous, and his head bandaged as if wounded. He wore a shabby jacket with tears in it which I had not noticed during the day. Full of an almost savage ardour he lifted and pushed the tables with a mad recklessness, smiling a little. He seemed to be playing some extraordinary game of his own of which we did not know the final word.

They arrived thus in the darkest corner of the room to move the last table.

In that place with a turn of his hand, Meaulnes could knock down his adversary without anyone outside being able to see or hear through the windows. I could not understand why he let this unique chance pass. The other, now near the door, would escape any moment on the pretext that the job was done and we would not see him again. The plan and all its' information which Meaulnes had taken so long to recover, match, and put together would be lost for ever...

Every moment I waited for my companion to give a sign or movement which would signal the beginning of the battle. But the big boy made no move. He just kept staring with a strange fixity and questioning air at the actor's bandage which in the half-light of nightfall seemed to be heavily smeared with black.

The last table was moved without anything happening.

But at the moment when they were both returning to the top of the classroom to give the doorstep its' last sweep of the broom, Meaulnes, lowering his head, and without looking at our enemy, said quietly,

"Your bandage is red with blood and your clothes are torn."

The other looked at him for a moment, not surprised at what he said but profoundly moved to hear him say it.

"They wanted to tear your plan from me just now in the square," he replied. "When they realized that I wanted to return and sweep the classroom they knew I wanted to make peace with you and they revolted against me. But I saved it from them all the same," he said fiercely, holding out to Meaulnes the precious folded paper.

Meaulnes turned slowly to me.

"Did you hear?" he said. "He has just been fighting and was wounded for us while we were setting a trap!"

Then ceasing to use the 'vous' unusual in the pupils of Sainte-Agathe:

"You are a true comrade," he said, and held out his hand.

The actor seized it wordlessly for a second, much troubled, his voice silenced...but soon he continued with ardent curiosity:

"So you were preparing a trap! How funny! I guessed that and thought how astonished they will be when they get back the plan and see that I have completed it"...

"Completed it?"

"Oh! Not entirely"...

Abandoning his light-hearted tone he added gravely and slowly as he approached us:

"Meaulnes, it's time I told you: I have also been where you went. I was also at that extraordinary party. I realised when the boys from the school told me about your mysterious adventure that it was connected with the old lost Domaine. To make sure I stole your map....but I am like you. I do not know the name of the chateau. I would not know how to return there. I do not know the whole route which took you from here to there."

With what eagerness, with what intense curiosity, and with what friendship we huddled together over it! Meaulnes asked eager questions...It seemed to both of us that by pressing close to our new friend so ardently we would make him tell us even what he claimed he did not know.

"You will see. You will see," the young man replied a little bored and embarrassed. "I have put some indications on the map which you did not have. That is all I could do."

Then seeing us so full of admiration and enthusiasm, he said sadly and proudly,

"I wanted to tell you. I'm not like the other boys. Three months ago I wanted to shoot myself in the head and that explains the bandage round my forehead like a soldier of the Seine in 1870..."

"And this evening while you were fighting the wound was reopened," said Meaulnes with friendship.

But the other, ignoring this, continued in a slow emphatic tone:

"I wanted to die. And since I did not succeed, I will continue to live only for amusement, like a child, like an actor. I have abandoned everything. I no longer have a father, nor a sister, nor a house, nor a lover...nothing except companions in play."

"Those companions have already betrayed you," I said.

"Yes," he replied with animation. "It is the fault of a certain Delouche. He discovered that I was going to make common cause with you. He has demoralized my gang which was being so well trained. You saw the attack yesterday evening. How well it went! Since my childhood I have not organized anything so successfully..."

He remained pondering for a moment, and then added, to clarify his position to us immediately,

"If I have come to you two this evening it is because I have realized since morning that there is more pleasure with you than with all the others put together. That Delouche above all disgusts me. What a farce to play the man at seventeen! Nothing disgusts me more...Do you think we can teach him a lesson?"

"Certainly," said Meaulnes, "but are you staying with us long?"

"I don't know. I'ld like to a lot. I'm terribly lonely. I've only got Ganache"...

All his fever, all his enjoyment, suddenly left him. In an instant he plunged into the same despair which no doubt had gripped him when the idea of killing himself had overtaken him."

And he added quite solemnly,

"Be my friends for the day when I may again be two fingers from hell as once before...Swear to me that you will respond when I call – when I call you like this," (and he gave a strange cry: Ooo-ooo!) "You, Meaulnes, swear first!"

And we swore, for, children that we were, all that was more solemn and serious than usual attracted us.

"In return," he said, "this is all that I can tell you at the moment. I will show you the house in Paris where the young girl from the chateau usually spends the festivals of Easter and Pentecost in June, and sometimes part of the Winter."

At that moment an unknown voice called from the main gate several times in the dark. We guessed that this was Ganache, the actor, who did not dare or did not know how to cross the yard. In an anxious urgent voice he called in a high-pitched voice, then in a low,

" Ooo-ooo! Ooo-ooo!"

"Tell me! Tell me quickly!" cried Meaulnes to the young actor who had shivered and was adjusting his clothes in order to leave.

The young man quickly gave us an address in Paris which we repeated quickly. Then he ran into the darkness to rejoin his companion at the gate, leaving us in a state of inexplicable agitation.

5.   The Man in Canvas Shoes

That night, towards three o'clock in the morning, the widow Delouche, the inn-keeper who lived in the centre of the town, got up to light her fire. Dumas, her brother-in-law, who lived with her, had to be on his way by four o'clock, and the miserable woman whose right hand was shriveled by an old burn, hastened to prepare coffee in the dark kitchen. It was cold. She wrapped an old shawl over her camisole and then took a lighted candle in one hand protecting the flame with the other - the bad one – and, her apron high, she crossed the yard which was cluttered with empty bottles and cases of soap, and opened the door of the woodshed which served also as a hen-coop, to take a little wood. Hardly had she closed the door when a cap exploded so violently that it made the air hum. Someone rushed out from the darkness, extinguished the candle and knocked down the old woman with one blow and escaped at full speed while the cocks and hens, driven crazy, created an infernal uproar.

The man carried away in his bag, as the widow Delouche noticed a moment too late as she recovered her wits, a dozen of her finest chickens.

At the cries of his sister-in-law Dumas ran to her. He established that the rogue, in order to enter, would have had to open the door of the small yard with a false key, and that he had escaped the same way closing it again. Used to poachers and thieves he immediately lit the lantern of his carriage and taking it in one hand, and his loaded rifle in the other, he tried to follow the tracks of the thief. These were very indistinct as the man must have been wearing canvass shoes. They led to the Station Road and were lost at the gate to the meadow. Forced to halt his pursuit there he raised his head and stopped...and heard in the distance on the same road the sound of a carriage at full gallop fleeing away....

Jasmin Delouche, the widow's son, had got up, hastily thrown a cloak round his shoulders, and gone outside in his slippers to inspect the town. Everything was asleep, everything plunged in darkness and the deep silence which precedes the first light of day. When he arrived at the crossroads he heard – like his uncle – very far away on the Riaudes hill the sound of a carriage whose horses must have galloped like the wind. Wicked and boastful boy as he was, he said to himself then, as he related to us later in his unbearable accent native to the suburbs of Montlucon,

"Those have gone towards the station, but that doesn't mean I won't smoke out others on the other side of the town."

And he resumed his walk towards the church in the same nocturnal silence.

In the square, in the actors' caravan, there was a light. Someone was ill probably. He approached to ask what had happened when a silent shadow, a shadow wearing canvass shoes, emerged from the Petite-Coins and ran up at a gallop without seeing anything, to the running-board of the caravan...

Jasmin, who had recognized the style of Ganache, advanced suddenly into the light and asked in a low voice,

"Well! What's going on?"

Haggard, disheveled and toothless, the other stopped, stared at him with a miserable grin caused by fear and lack of breath, and replied in a jerky voice,

"It's my companion who is ill...he had a fight yesterday and his wound has reopened...I have just been to look for the sister."

And in fact as Jasmin Delouche, very intrigued, returned home to go back to bed, he met in the middle of the town a nun in great haste.

In the morning many of the townsfolk of Sainte-Agathe went out on to their doorsteps, their eyes puffed and shadowed after a night without sleep. They were all raising a cry of indignation through the town like a trail of powder.

At Giraudat's house they had heard around two o'clock a small cart which stopped, and it had been packed hastily with packets which fell softly. In the house there had been only two women and they had not dared to move. In the morning they had realised when they opened the poultry yard that the 'packets' were rabbits and poultry...Millie, during the first recreation found in front of the door to the wash-house a lot of half-burnt matches. We thought the intruders had been ill-informed about our house and had not been able to enter...At Perreux' house, at Boujardins' and at Clemonts' they thought at first pigs had also been stolen, but they were recovered during the morning busily digging up lettuces in other peoples' gardens. The whole herd had taken advantage of the occasion and the open doors to do a little nocturnal expedition...Practically everywhere poultry had been stolen; but the affair did not stop at that. Mme. Pignot, the baker's wife, who did not have live-stock, complained all day that someone had stolen her washing-tub and a packet of indigo, but this could neither be proved nor written in the report...

The panic, the fear, the gossip, lasted the whole morning. In class Jasmin recounted his adventure of the night:

"They are crooks," he said, "but if my uncle had met one, he says he would have shot him like a rabbit!"

And he added, looking at us,

"It's a good job he did not meet Ganache. He would have been capable of shooting him down. They all belong to the same race he said, and Dessaigne said the same."

Meanwhile no-one dreamed of suspecting our new friends. It wasn't till the evening of the next day that Jasmin remarked to his uncle that Ganache wore canvass shoes like the thief. They agreed it was worth the trouble of telling this to the police. They decided secretly therefore to go as soon as they had time to the county town of the Canton to inform the Chief Inspector of Police.

During the days which followed, the young actor, sick from his open wound, did not appear..

In the church square, in the evenings, we would prowl around, simply to see the lamp behind the red curtain of the caravan. Full of a feverish distress we remained there, without daring to approach the humble dwelling, which to us seemed like the antechamber and path to the country the way to which we had lost.

6.   A Dispute in the Wings

So many anxieties and troubles of different sorts had prevented us noticing that March had arrived and that the wind had softened. But the third day after this adventure when I went down in the morning to the yard I realized with a shock that it was Spring. A delicious breeze like warm water blew over the wall; silent rain had moistened the peony leaves in the night. The reviving earth in the garden had a pungent smell, and in a tree close to the window I heard a bird trying to learn music...

Meaulnes, at the first recreation, spoke of trying straight away to follow the plan which the actor-pupil had clarified for us. With great difficulty I persuaded him to wait until we had met our friend again, and until the weather was set definitely fair...until all Sainte-Agathe was in flower. Leaning against the low wall of the little alley, our hands in our pockets and bare-headed, we talked and the wind made us shiver sometimes with cold and then enveloping us with warmth and reawakening in us, I can't describe what profound eagerness, as of old. Ah! Brother, companion, traveler, how convinced we were that happiness was just close by, and we had only to set off to attain it!...

At half-past, during lunch, we heard the rolling of drums in the cross-roads square. In a flash we were on the step of the small gate, our napkins in our hands...It was Ganache announcing that that evening at eight o'clock if the weather was fine there would be an entertainment in the church square. In any case a tent would be erected in case of rain. There followed the long programme of attractions which the wind carried away, but we could make out that there would be 'miming', 'singing', 'horse-riding tricks', the whole of it was emphasized by a fresh roll of drums.

During dinner that evening, the large cash-box was shaken under our windows to announce the event, making the window-panes tremble. Soon after, people coming in from the suburbs in small groups, with their bombardment of talk, passed by on their way to

92

the church square. And we were there, both of us, forced to remain at table, our feet stamping with impatience!

Towards nine o'clock, at last, we heard shuffling of feet and silent laughter by the small gate. The school-teachers had come to look for us. We left together in complete darkness for the place where the show was to be held. In the distance we saw the wall of the church illumined as by a great fire. Two hurricane lamps which had been lit hung by the opening to the tent and swayed in the wind...

Inside, steps had been arranged as in a circus. M. Seurel, the teachers, Meaulnes and I installed ourselves in the front row. I can see now that interior which must have been very narrow, looking like a real circus with deep shadowed areas where Mme. Pignot, the baker's wife, and Fernande, the grocer's wife, girls from the town, labourers from the blacksmith's, women, boys, peasants and others were seated.

The performance was more than half-way through. In the rink there was a little goat doing tricks. Quite docilely it placed its' feet on four glasses, then on two, and then on one. It was Ganache who was directing it gently with taps from a small stick, while looking towards us in a worried manner, his mouth open, his eyes dead.

Seated on a stool close to two other lamps in the place where the floor communicated with the caravan, we recognized in the fine close-fitting black jersey, his forehead bound, the ring-master, our friend.

Hardly were we seated than a fully-harnessed pony bounded into the ring. The wounded young personage made it do several rounds. It had to stop in front of the one of us who was most amiable or the most brave of the audience; but it was always in front of Mme. Pignot that it stopped when it was a case of 'the biggest liar', 'the most miserly', or 'the most amorous'...And it was round her that the shouts of laughter, cries and hoots went up, like a flock of geese chased by a spaniel!...

At the interval, the ring-master came to talk for a moment with M. Seurel who could not have been more proud if he had talked with a Talma or a Leotard; and as for us, we listened with passionate interest to all that he said; about his wound – closed again; about the show – prepared during the last days of Winter; about their departure

– which would not be before the end of the month as they were thinking of giving a variety of new shows till then.

The programme would end with a grand pantomime.

Towards the end of the interval our friend left us and in order to reach the entrance of the caravan was obliged to pass by a group which had invaded the ring, in the middle of which we suddenly saw Jasmin Delouche. The women and girls moved aside. His black costume, and wounded air which was both mysterious and brave had charmed everyone. As for Jasmin, who looked as if he had returned that moment from a journey, and was talking in a low animated tone with Mme. Pignot, it was obvious that a girdle, low collar, and elephant pantaloons would have suited his triumph more aptly...He kept his thumbs in the lapels of his jacket, in a foppish and yet very awkward manner. As the actor passed through, in a movement of annoyance he said something in a loud voice to Mme. Pignot. I could not hear it but it was certainly an insult or something provocative intended for our friend. It must have been a serious and unexpected threat because the young man could not help turning and looking at the other, who in order not to lose his sneering countenance, nudged his neighbours with his elbows as if to include them on his side..All this however passed in a few seconds. I was certainly the only one on our bench to have seen it.

The ring-master rejoined his companion behind the curtain which hid the entrance to the caravan. Everyone went back to his place on the steps expecting the second part of the show to commence immediately, and complete silence was established. Then, behind the curtain, as the last quiet conversations ended, the sound of a dispute ensued. We did not hear what was said but we recognized the two voices, that of the large fellow and that of the young man – the first explaining something to justify himself, the other scolding in a mixture if indignation and distress.

"But for goodness sake!" said the latter, "Why didn't you tell me..."

We could not make out the rest although everyone was straining his ears. Then suddenly all went quiet. The altercation continued in low voices, and the small boys on the top steps began to chant:

"Lights! Curtain!" And to stamp their feet."

7. The Actor Takes off his Bandage

At last, between the curtains, the face appeared slowly, of a tall Pierrot, his features ploughed with wrinkles which stretched first in a parody of gaiety and then of anguish. His body seemed to form three badly-articulated parts bent at the stomach as if with colic. He walked on the tips of his toes in an excess of prudence or fear, his hands tangled in sleeves which were so long that they swept the floor.

I cannot reconstruct the subject of the pantomime. I can remember only that after his arrival in the ring he tried vainly to keep on his feet but always fell. No matter how hard he tried to stand up it was too much for him and he would fall again. He fell incessantly. He got himself tied up in four chairs at once and in his fall he dragged down a large table which had been brought into the ring. He ended up stretched out beyond the barrier of the ring at the feet of the spectators. Two assistants enlisted with great difficulty from the audience pulled him with inconceivable difficulty back on to his feet. And each time he fell he gave a little cry in which distress and satisfaction were mixed in equal doses. At the end, having climbed on to a scaffolding of chairs, he slid down slowly from the top and his shrill howl of triumph was accompanied by cries of fear from some of the women.

During the second part of his pantomime I saw "the poor falling pierrot" again, I can't remember why, drawing out from one of his sleeves a little doll stuffed with bran, and with it he mimed a whole scene of tragi-comedy. Finally he made all the bran in its' stomach come out through its' mouth. Then with pitiful cries he restuffed it with gruel, and when everyone's attention was fixed, mouths open, on the sticky doll, torn by the poor pierrot, he suddenly seized it by one arm and threw it with all his strength over the spectators at Jasmin Delouche. It merely wet his ear and went on to land on the stomach of Mme. Pignot just under her chin. The baker's wife gave a loud cry and fell over backwards so heavily that all her neighbours followed her example. The bench broke and the baker's wife, Fernande, the sad widow Delouche, and twenty others all fell down, their legs in the air, to the shouts of laughter and applause, while the great clown fell on his face on the ground. He raised himself again to take his leave and say:

"We have, ladies and gentlemen, the honour of thanking you all so much!"

But at that moment in the middle of the general din big Meaulnes, silent from the beginning of the pantomime and growing more preoccupied by the minute, suddenly rose and seized me by the arm as if unable to contain himself.

"Look at the actor!" he cried. "Look! At last I have recognised him."

Before even looking, as if the idea had brooded inside me unconsciously for a long time, waiting only for the occasion to burst upon me, I had understood! Standing near a light by the entrance, the unknown young man had removed his bandage and thrown a cape round his shoulders. He could be seen now in the smoky light just as he had appeared formerly by candle-light in the room of the Domaine, his face very fine and aquiline without a moustache. Pale, his lips parted, he leafed hastily through some little red albumn which must have been a pocket atlas. Save for a scar which crossed his temple and disappeared under the mass of hair, he was just as he had been described to me so minutely by big Meaulnes, the fiancé of the lost Domaine.

It was clear that he had removed his bandage in order to be recognised by us. But hardly had Meaulnes stood up and cried out than the young man retreated into the caravan. He glanced towards us first however with a look of understanding, and smiled with the same vague sorrow that always marked his smile.

"And the other one!" said Meaulnes feverishly. "How was it I didn't recognize him immediately? It is the Pierrot from the Fete down there"...

And he went down the steps towards him. But Ganache had already cut off all his communications with the ring. One by one he was extinguishing the four lanterns round the circle, and we were obliged to follow the crowd making its way slowly between the parallel benches in the dark. We stamped our feet in impatience.

As soon as he was at last outside big Meaulnes rushed to the caravan, climbed the steps and knocked on the door, but everything was already locked up. Probably already in the curtained vehicle, as in the one for the pony, the goat, and the performing birds, everyone had retired and was about to sleep.

8. The Police!

We had to rejoin the troop of ladies and gentlemen returning towards the school by the dark roads. Now we understood everything. The large white silhouette which Meaulnes had seen the last evening of the Fete passing through the trees was Ganache who had gathered up the desperate fiancé and was fleeing away with him. The other had accepted the savage existence, full of risks and games of adventure. It seemed to recapture his childhood...

Frantz de Galais had hidden his name from us till now, and had pretended to be ignorant of the road to the Domaine, for fear no doubt that he would be forced to return to his parents; but why suddenly had he wanted to make himself known to us that evening and allow us to realise the whole truth?...

What plans did big Meaulnes not make as the troop of spectators walked slowly back to the town! He decided that the next morning which was Thursday he would go and find Frantz. And both of them would set off to go back there! What a journey it would be along that wet road! Frantz would explain everything. Everything would be settled and the marvelous adventure would take him back to where it had been interrupted...

As for me I walked along in the darkness with an indefinable swelling of the heart. Everything had combined to contribute to my joy, from the first small pleasure of waiting for Thursday to the very great discovery which we were about to make, or to the very great risk that we would be defeated. And I remember that in my sudden generosity of heart I approached the ugliest of the notary's daughters, to whom I had once had the torture of being forced to offer my arm, and spontaneously offered my hand.

Bitter recollection! Vain crushed hope!

The next day at eight o'clock we emerged, the two of us, into the church square with our shoes well polished, the buckles of our belts shining, and wearing new caps. Meaulnes, who up till then had kept from smiling when he looked at me, uttered a cry and rushed into the empty square...In the place where the shed and the vehicles had stood there was only a broken pot and some rags. The actors had left...

A breeze which seemed icy to us blew around us. It seemed to me that at every step we would fall and strike the hard stony ground of the square. Meaulnes, absolutely wild, made two movements as if to throw himself first along the road to Vieux-Nancy, then along the road to Loup des Bois. He put his hand over his eyes hoping for a moment that our people had only just left. Bur there was nothing to be done. The traces of ten vehicles were all mixed in the square, only to be lost on the hard road. We had to stand there, helpless.

And as we turned back to the village where Thursday morning was beginning, four policemen on horse-back, informed by Delouche the evening before, galloped into the square. Then they separated along the various roads to guard all exits like dragons reconnoitering the village...But it was too late. Ganache, the stealer of chickens, had fled with his companion. The police found no-one, neither him, nor the carts with the captives which he had strangled. Warned in time by an imprudent word from Jasmin, Frantz must suddenly have understood his companion's trade and what kept them going when the cash-box of the caravan was empty; full of shame and fury he had stopped the itinerary immediately and decided to escape the countryside before the arrival of the police. But not afraid any more that someone would try and take him back to his father's Domaine, he had wanted to show himself to us without his bandage before disappearing.

One point only remained obscure. How had Ganache managed to rob the poultry-yards, and at the same time persuade the nun to treat his friend's fever? Yet wasn't that like the whole story of the poor creature? Thief and tramp on the one hand, and good fellow on the other.

9. In Search of the Lost Path

As we returned the sun dispersed the light morning mist and the various households were busy on the doorsteps of their houses shaking out their carpets and gossiping: and in the fields and woods as far as the doors of the town there began the most radiant Spring of my recollection.

All the senior pupils of the Course had to arrive at about eight o'clock that Thursday to prepare that morning for their Senior Certificate of Studies, or for the Teachers' Training Examination. When we two arrived Meaulnes was so full of grief that he could not keep still. I was also very upset. The school was empty...A ray of sunlight slid on to the dust of the worm-eaten bench and on to the flaking varnish of the globe.

How could we stay there in front of a book thinking only of our disappointment while everything called us outside; the flight of the birds in the branches close to the windows; the flight of the other pupils to the fields and the woods; and above all the feverish desire to try out as quickly as possible the incomplete map which the actor had clarified a little – the last resource of our almost empty bag, the last key of the bunch when we had tried all the others?...That was beyond our resources! Meaulnes strode to and fro, went to the window, looked into the garden, then returned and looked towards the town as if he was watching for someone who certainly would not come.

"I have an idea," he said at last. "I think it may not be as far as we imagine...

"On my plan Frantz has deleted a whole section of road which I had marked in...

"That means maybe that while I was asleep the mare made a long detour..."

I was half-seated on a corner of the big table, one foot on the ground, the other swinging in a discouraged and idle manner, my head lowered.

"Still," I said, "on your return in the berlin your journey had lasted all night."

"We left at midnight," he said eagerly. "I was dropped at four o'clock in the morning about six kilometres west of Sainte-Agathe, whereas I had left by the road to the east of the station. So we have to count those six kilometers off the distance between Sainte- Agathe and the lost Domaine. Really it seems to me that after leaving the Communaux woods it should not be more than two miles to the place we are looking for."

"And it is precisely those two miles which are missing from the map."

"Yes, and the way out of the woods is a good four and a half miles from here, but for a good walker it can be done in a morning".

At that moment Moucheboeuf arrived. He had an irritating habit of passing for a good student, not by working better than the others, but by attracting attention to himself in circumstances such as these.

"I knew I would find you two here," he said triumphantly. "All the others have left for the Communaux woods, at the head Jasmin Delouche who knows where the nests are."

And wishing to prove himself a good apostle he proceeded to recount all that they had said to defy the school, M. Seurel, and ourselves in planning the expedition.

"If they are in the woods I shall no doubt see them as I pass," said Meaulnes, "because I am going there too. I will be back about twelve-thirty."

Moucheboeuf was astounded.

"Aren't you coming?" Augustin asked me as he paused for a second on the threshold of the open door – the one which gave entrance to the grey room, bringing a tide of air warmed by the sun, and a mixture of cries, calls, and chirpings, the sound of a bucket on the ledge of the well, and the crack of a whip in the distance.

"No," I said, though the temptation was strong, "I can't because of M. Seurel. But don't take long. I shall be waiting impatiently."

He made a vague gesture, and left hurriedly, full of hope.

When M. Seurel arrived at about ten o'clock he had left off his black alpaca jacket and put on a fishing coat with vast buttoned pockets, a straw hat, and short varnished leggings to hold in the

101

bottoms of his baggy pants. I knew very well that he was hardly surprised at finding no-0ne. He did not want to listen to Moucheboeuf who repeated to him three times what the boys had said:

"If he wants us let him come and find us!"

And he ordered:

"Get ready, put on your caps, and we will go and track them down...Can you walk so far Francois?"

I said yes and we left.

It was decided that Mouchebouef would lead M. Seurel and act as a decoy...that meant that since he knew the trees where the birds' nesters would be found he would shout out from time to time:

"Hey! Hello! Giraudat! Delouche! Where are you?...Have you found any?"

As for me I was charged to my great delight with the job of following round the perimeter of the wood in case any run-away students tried to escape from that side.

For in the plan which the actor had corrected and which I had studied so many times with Meaulnes there seemed to be a track or a footpath which followed the boundary of the wood to go in the direction of the Domaine. Suppose I discovered it that morning!....I began to persuade myself that before mid-day I would discover the path to the lost manor...

What a marvelous walk!...As soon as we had passed the Glacis and rounded the mill, I left my two companions, M. Seurel about whom one could only say that he had set off ready to do battle, and the traitor Mouchebouef.

Taking a road at right-angles I will arrive soon at the edge of the wood – walking across the countryside for the first time in my life like a man on patrol lost by his corporal.

Here I am, I imagine, full of that mysterious happiness which Meaulnes had experienced once before. The whole of the morning is mine to explore the edge of the wood, the freshest and most hidden place of the area, while my great friend is also on the great journey of discovery. The path seems to be an ancient stream bed. I pass under the low branches of trees whose names I do not know, but which must be alders. After a while I jump over a fence at the end of the path and find myself in a wide lane of green grass under the leaves, treading sometimes on nettles crushing the tall valerians.

Sometimes my foot treads for a few paces on a bank of fine sand. And in the silence I hear a bird – I imagine it is a nightingale, but no doubt I am mistaken since they sing only in the evening – a bird which repeats the same phrase persistently: the voice of the morning, a word spoken in the shadows, a delicious invitation to a journey between the alders. Invisible, obstinate, it seems to accompany me under the leaves.

For the first time here am I, I too, on the road to adventure. It's no more lost shells, abandoned by birds, which I am looking for under the direction of M. Seurel, nor orchids which the school-master does not recognise, nor even like that search we had in Pierre Martin's field.

There was a deep dried-up spring there covered by a grate but it was invisible under the rank foliage and each time it took longer to find it...I am looking for something much more mysterious. It is the path one reads about in books, the ancient hidden way, the entrance to which the prince, worn down by exhaustion, cannot discover. It is found only when all account of time is lost, whether it is eleven o'clock, mid-day...And suddenly while parting the branches in the dense undergrowth with hesitating hands, he glimpses through the gaps in the foliage, what seems to be a long dark avenue which ends in a tiny circle of light.

But while I hope and am thus intoxicated I emerge suddenly into a sort of clearing which proves to be only a field. I have arrived without even thinking about it at the edge of the Communaux which I had always imagined to be infinitely far away. And here on my right between piles of wood, humming in the shade, is the game-keeper's lodge. Two pairs of stockings are drying on the window-sill. In former years when we arrived at the entrance to the wood we would always say, pointing to a small light at the end of a very long dark footpath,

"Down there is the game-keeper's lodge, Baladier's house." But we never continued that far, we would hear said sometimes, as if someone had completed an extraordinary expedition,

"He has been as far as the game-keeper's lodge!"

This time I have come as far as Baladier's house and I have found nothing.

I began to suffer with my tired leg and the heat which I had not been aware of till then. I was afraid to attempt the return journey by myself, and then heard close-by M. Seurel's decoy, Moucheboeuf, then other voices calling me...

There was a gang of six big boys, among whom only the traitor Moucheboeuf wore a triumphant air. They were Giraudat, Auberger, Delage and others... Thanks to the decoy some had been caught climbing an isolated cherry-tree in the middle of a clearing; others were busy searching for the nest of woodpeckers. Giraud, the fool with puffy eyes and a dirty shirt, had hidden fledglings against his stomach between his shirt and his skin. Two of his companions had fled at the approach of M. Seurel. They must have been Delouche and little Coffin. They had already responded with jokes addressed to "Mouchevache", the sounds of which echoes in the wood, and he, sure of his ground but clumsy, had replied in vexed tones,

"You've only got to come down you know! M. Seurel is here"...

Then suddenly everything went quiet; it was a flight of silence across the wood. And as they knew him so well it was useless to think of catching up with them. No-one knew if Meaulnes had passed that way. No-one had heard his voice, and we had to give up any further search for them.

It was after mid-day when we regained the road to Sainte-Agathe, slowly, heads down, weary and muddy. At the entrance to the wood when we had rubbed our shoes and shaken off the mud on the dry road the sun began to beat down. Already it was no longer a fresh and shining Spring morning. The sounds of the afternoon had begun. Away in the distance a cock crowed, (a desolate cry!) In the deserted far-yards surrounding our route. At the Glacis hill we stopped for a moment to talk to one of the farm-labourers who had resumed their work after lunch. They were leaning on the gate and M. Seurel said for their benefit,

"Fine ragamuffins you are! Look at Giraudat. He put baby birds inside his shirt and they have done what they wanted to do in there. Naturally!"...

It seemed as if it was my downfall too at which the labourers laughed. They laughed with their heads shaking but they did not altogether blame us boys whom they knew well. They even confided to us when M. Seurel resumed his place in the lead,

"Another boy came by this way too, a big boy, you know him....he must have met the Granges carriage and they gave him a lift on his way home. He got down here, covered with earth and his clothes torn, at the beginning of the road to the Granges. We told him that we had seen you pass by this morning but that you hadn't returned yet. And he went on slowly along the road to Sainte-Agathe."

As it turned out we came across big Meaulnes sitting on the wall of the bridge of Glacis. He seemed broken with fatigue. In reply to M. Seurel's questions he said he had also gone in search of truant students. And to one I asked him quietly, he shook his head in discouragement,

"No! Nothing! Nothing that looked like that."

After lunch in the closed classroom, now dark and empty in the middle of the radiant countryside, he sat at one of the big tables with his head in his arms. He remained there for a long time in a sad deep sleep. Towards evening, after a long moment of thought, as if he had come to an important decision, he wrote to his mother. And that is all I can remember of that dismal end to a long day of defeat.

10. The Washing

We had anticipated Spring too early.

On Monday evening we wanted to do our homework immediately after four o'clock as we did in Summer, and in order to see it clearly we put two tables out into the yard. But the day suddenly darkened; a drop of rain fell on an exercise-book; we retreated in haste. And in the large dim room we stood silently by the big windows watching the clouds sailing by in the grey sky.

Then Meaulnes who was watching as we were, his hand on the window-handle, could not help saying as if he was angry with himself for feeling so much regret,

"Ah! The clouds sailed differently when I was going along in the Belle-Etoile carriage."

"On which road?" asked Jasmin.

But Meaulnes did not reply.

In order to create a diversion I said,

"I would have loved to travel like that in a carriage in the driving rain under a great umbrella."

"And read all the way, just as at home," said another.

"It wasn't raining and I didn't want to read," said Meaulnes. "I just watched the countryside."

But when Giraudat asked, in his turn, what countryside, Meaulnes remained silent again. And Jasmin said,

"I know...always the same adventure!"...

He said these words in a conciliatory and self-important way as if he was also partly in the secret. It was a lost labour. His advances achieved nothing; and as night fell everyone ran off at a gallop with his shirt pulled up over his head in the cold downpour.

The rain continued until Thursday. And that Thursday was even worse than the preceeding one. The whole countryside was bathed in a sort of icy mist like in the worst days of Winter.

Millie, deceived by the fine sunshine of the week before, had done the washing, but one could not think of putting the clothes on the hedges in the garden to dry, nor even on lines in the attic. The air was too cold and damp.

When she discussed it with M. Seurel he had the idea of spreading the washing in the classroom since it was Thursday, and of heating the stove on full. To economise on fires in the kitchen and in the dining-room the food would be cooked on the stove and we would spend the day in the classroom.

For a moment – I was so young still! – I thought of this novelty as like a festival.

Dreary festival!...All the heat of the stove was absorbed by the washing and it was very cold. In the yard a soft Winter drizzle fell interminably. However it was there at nine o'clock in the morning, and eaten up with boredom, I found Meaulnes again. By the bars of the main gate where we leant our heads silently, we watched at the end of the town at the Four-Routes the arrival of a cortege. It had come in from the countryside for burial. The coffin which had been brought in on an ox-cart was taken out and placed on the pavement at the foot of the great cross where a short while ago the butcher had seen the actor's two sentinels! Where was he now, the young captain who had led the charge so well?....The priest and the two precentors went ahead as usual in front of the coffin and the sad hymns could be heard where we were. We knew it would be the only diversion of the day which would pass otherwise like a yellow stream into a gutter.

"And now," said Meaulnes suddenly, "I have to pack. Listen Seurel, I wrote to mother last Thursday to ask her to let me finish my studies in Paris. I leave today."

He continued looking towards the town, his hands resting on the bars level with his head. No need to ask whether his mother who was rich and who granted all his wishes had granted this one also. No need to ask why he suddenly wanted to go to Paris!...

But there was in him certainly regret and fear of leaving this dear place of Sainte-Agathe from where he had left for his adventure. As for me I experienced a sense of violent desolation such as I had never known before.

"It will soon be Easter!" he said in explanation with a sigh.

"As soon as you get there you will write to me, won't you?" I asked.

"That is a promise, for sure. Aren't you my companion and my brother?"...

And he put his hand on my shoulder.

Gradually I realised that this was really the end, because he would finish his studies in Paris; I would never again have my great comrade with me.

There was no hope of our reunion except in that house in Paris where he must recover the traces of his lost adventure...But to see Meaulnes himself so unhappy, what poor hope was there for me?

My parents were informed: M Seurel was astounded but gave way to the reasons Meaulnes put forward; Millie, housewife, was most worried at the thought of Meaulnes' mother seeing her house in such unaccustomed disorder..The trunk alas was soon packed. We searched under the stairs for his Sunday shoes, in the wardrobe for an under-garment; then his papers and school-books – all that a young man of eighteen possesses in the world.

At mid-day Mme. Meaulnes arrived with the carriage. She lunched at Daniel's café in company with Augustin, and took him away with hardly any explanation as soon as the horse was fed and harnessed. On the doorstep we bade him farewell; and the carriage disappeared round the corner of Four-Routes.

Millie rubbed her shoes at the door and returned to the cold dining-room to tidy up all that had been disarranged. As for me I found myself for the first time in many months alone to face a long Thursday evening with the feeling that in that old carriage my adolescence was disappearing for ever.

11.   I Betray

What was I to do?

The weather lifted a little. It even seemed as if the sun was going to come out.

A door would bang in the great house. Then silence would fall again. From time to time my father crossed the yard to fill a bucket with charcoal with which he stuffed the stove. I saw white clothes hanging on the lines and I had no desire to go back into that melancholy place transformed now into a drying room, to find myself face to face with the end of year examination, this Teachers' Training Course which henceforth was to be my only preoccupation.

It was strange: the devastating boredom was mixed with a sense of freedom. Meaulnes was gone, the whole adventure ended and lost, but it seemed at least that I was liberated from the strange anxiety, the mysterious obsession which would not allow me to behave like all the rest of the world. Meaulnes gone I was no longer his companion in adventures, the brother of a hunter of trails. I became again a boy of the town like the others. And that was easy and I had only to follow my most natural inclination.

The younger boy of the Roy family passed by in the muddy road swinging three chestnuts on the end of a string and then tossing them into the air so that they landed in the school-yard. My holiday mood was so great that I took pleasure in throwing the chestnuts back to him two or three times from the other side of the wall.

Suddenly I saw him abandon the childish game to run towards a cart which was coming along the road from Vieille-Planche. He jumped on to it quickly from behind without the cart even stopping. I recognised the cart as that of Delouche, and his horse. Jasmin was driving; fat Boujardon was standing in it. They were coming back from the fields.

"Come with us Francois!" cried Jasmin, who must have known that Meaulnes had left.

My goodness, without informing anyone, I climbed into the jolting vehicle and behaved like the others, standing and leaning against one of the upright posts of the cart. It took us to widow Delouche's house…

We are now in the back room of the good woman's shop who was both a grocer and an inn-keeper. A ray of sunlight slides across the low window-pane on to the tin boxes and the barrels of vinegar. Fat Boujardin is seated on the window-sill and turns towards us and with the thick laugh if a pasty man he eats biscuits with a spoon. Within reach of his hand on a barrel a box is opened and started. The young boy gives cries of pleasure. A sort of intimacy of a dubious kind is established between us. Jasmin and Boujardon are now my companions I observe. The course of my life has suddenly changed. It seems as if Meaulnes has been gone a long time and that his adventure is an old story, sad but finished..

Little Roy has unearthed from under a plank an opened bottle of liqueur. Delouche offers a drop to each of us but there is only one glass and we all drink from it. I am served first with a little condescension as if I am not accustomed to the habits of hunters and peasants…This embarrasses me a little. And when they begin to talk of Meaulnes I am seized with a desire to get rid of my embarrassment and recover my poise by showing that I know his story and telling a bit of it. How can this harm him since all his adventures here are now finished now?…

Am I telling this story badly? It does not produce the effect I expected. My companions like good villagers whom nothing astonishes are not surprised by so little.

"It was a marriage was it?" says Boujardon. Delouche has seen one in Preveranges which was even more curious.

The chateau? One would certainly find people of the district who have heard speak of it.

The young girl? Meaulnes will marry her when he has done his years' service.

"He should have told us," adds one of them, "and shown us the map instead of trusting it to an actor!"…

Tangled in my failure I want to take advantage of the occasion to excite their curiosity. I decide to explain who the actor was and where he came from; his strange destiny…Boujardon and Delouche do not want to listen:

110

"It's he who was responsible for everything. It was he who made Meaulnes unsociable, Meaulnes who was such a good friend! It was he who organized all those foolish boardings and night-time attacks after recruiting us like a school battalion..."

"You know," says Jasmin looking at Boujardon and shaking his head with little jerks, "I did well in denouncing his so harshly to the police. There was someone who had harmed the countryside and would do it again!"...

Here I am almost of their opinion. Everything would have turned out differently if we had not viewed the affair in such a mysterious and tragic a fashion. It is the influence of Frantz which has lost us everything...

But suddenly while I am absorbed in these reflections there is a noise in the shop. Jasmin Delouche quickly hides his flask of brandy behind a barrel; fat Boujardon tumbles from the window-sill, puts his foot on an empty dust y bottle which rolls and escapes twice from a sprawl. Little Roy pushes them from behind to get out quickly, half-suffocated with laughter.

Without understanding exactly what is happening I run away with them. We cross the yard and climb by a ladder into a loft full of hay. I hear a woman's voice treating us like good-for-nothings!...

"I wouldn't have believed she would have returned so soon," says Jasmin in a low voice.

I realise only now that we are here under false pretences, to steal cake and wine. I have been deceived like the castaway who thought he was talking to a man and recognized suddenly that it was a monkey. I think only of leaving the loft, for such adventures don't please me at all. Besides it is getting dark..I am let out the back way across two gardens and round a pond, and find myself in the wet muddy road where the light of Daniel's café is reflected.

I am not proud of my evening. I find myself at the Four-Routes. In spite of myself, all of a sudden, I see again at the turning a hard brotherly face smiling at me; a last wave of the hand – and the carriage disappears.

A cold wind makes my shirt flap, like the wind of this Winter which was so tragic and yet so fine. Already everything appears less simple. In the big classroom where they are waiting for me for dinner

111

sharp currents of air cross the feeble warmth coming from the stove. I shiver while they reproach me for my afternoon's vagabondage. I do not even have in returning to the regularity of the former life the consolation of taking my place at table and getting back my usual seat. The table is not set this evening. Everyone eats on his knees as best he can in the dim classroom. I eat the flat cake baked in the stove silently. This is to be the recompense for a Thursday spent in school, and it is burnt in red circles.

At night, alone in my room, I sleep quickly to stifle the remorse which I can feel rising in the depths of my sorrow. But twice I am awakened in the middle of the night, thinking I can hear, the first time the creaking in the neighbouring bed where Meaulnes was in the habit of rolling over suddenly in one piece, and the next time his soft tread like a hunter on the lookout across the darkness of the attics...

12. Meaulnes' Three Letters

In my whole life I have received only three letters from Meaulnes.. I still have them in a drawer. Each time I re-read them I experience the same sadness as then.

The first arrived the second day after his departure.

My dear Francois,

Today as soon as I arrived in Paris I went to see that house. I saw nothing. There was no-one there. There never will be anyone.

The house which Frantz told us about is a small hotel with one floor. Melle de Galais' room must be on the first floor. The upper windows are hidden by the trees. But while passing by on the pavement they can be seen very well. All the curtains are closed and one would have to be mad to hope that one day from between the closed curtains the face of Yvonne de Galais could appear.

It is on a boulevard...It was raining a little on the trees which are already green. One can hear the clear bells of passing trams indistinctly.

For nearly two hours I walked to and fro under the windows. There is a wine-seller and I stopped there to drink so I would not be suspected of being a robber planning a raid. Then I resumed my watch without hope.

Night came. Lights went on in some of the windows round about but not in that house. There is certainly no-one there. And yet Easter is approaching.

As I was about to leave a young girl, or young woman - I don't know – came to sit on one of the benches, wet with rain. She was dressed in black with a white collar. When I had gone she remained there, immobile in spite of the cold of the evening, to wait for, I don't know what, I don't know what. You see that Paris is full of fools like me.

Augustin.

Time passed. In vain I waited for a word from Augustin on Easter Monday, and every day following - days when it seemed after the great fever of Easter, that there was no longer anything to wait for except the Summer. June brought examination time and a terrible heat. Its' suffocating humidity covered the surrounding countryside without a breath of wind to dispel it. Night brought no freshness and therefore no respite from the torture. It was during that insupportable month of June that I received the second letter from Meaulnes.

My dear Friend,

This time all hope is lost. I have known it since yesterday evening. The grief which I could hardly take in at once has been rising since then.

Every evening I would go and sit on that bench, reflecting, hoping in spite of everything. People gossiped on the pavement under the trees. Above, the dark foliage, made green by the lights. The second and third floor apartments were lit up. Here and there was a window which had been opened wide because of the Summer. One would see a lamp, illuminated on a table, hardly managing to hold back the dark heat of June. One could see almost to the back of the room...Ah! If the black window belonging to Yvonne de Galais had been lit like that, I would have dared I think, to climb the steps, to knock, to enter...

The young girl about whom I told you was there again, watching like me. I thought she must know the house and I asked her,

" – I know," she said, "that once a young girl and her brother used to come to spend their holidays there. But I have heard that the brother ran away from his parents' chateau and no-one could find him, and that the young girl is married. That explains why the apartment is closed."

I left. After about ten paces my feet stumbled on the pavement and I almost fell. The night - that is last night – when at last the women and children were quiet in the yards, allowing me to sleep, I began to hear carriages rolling along the road. They passed by in the distance. But when one had passed, in spite of myself, I waited for the next: the bell, the steps of the horse clacking on the asphalt...each would repeat: the town is deserted, your love is lost, the night interminable, the Summer, the fever...

Seurel, my friend, I am in great distress.

Augustin.

114

Letters of little confidence however you view them! Meaulnes spoke neither of why he had remained silent so long nor of what he intended to do now. I had the impression that he was breaking with me, as he was breaking with his past. No matter how I wrote to him I received no more response, only a word of felicitation when I received my preliminary teaching diploma. In September I knew through a school-friend that he had come to his mother's house in La Ferte-d'Angillon for the holidays. But that year we had been invited by my Uncle Florentin of Vieux-Nancay to spend the holidays with him. And Meaulnes departed for Paris without my being able to see him.

On my return towards the end of November, while I was full of a dejected enthusiasm to prepare for my Senior Diploma, in the hope of qualifying as a teacher the next year without going to the school in Bourges, I received the last of the three letters which I have ever received from Meaulnes:

"I still walk under that window," he wrote. "I still wait without the least hope, only folly. At the end of these cold Autumn Sundays, as night approaches I cannot make up my mind to return home and close the shutters of my room, without going back there, in the freezing road.

I am like that mad woman of Sainte-Agathe who used to go out every minute on to the doorstep and look with her hand above her eyes towards the station to see if her son who was dead was coming.

Seated on the bench, trembling and miserable, I like to imagine that someone is going to take me gently by the arm…I will turn. It will be she. "I am a little late," she will say simply. And all pain and all madness will vanish. We will enter our house. Her furs are icy, her veil wet; she brings with her the taste of the outdoor mist, and when she approaches the fire I see her blond hair covered with frost, her beautiful profile, so delicately designed, leaning towards the flame…

Alas! The window-pane remains opaque because of the curtain behind it. And even if the young girl from the lost Domaine were to open it I no longer have anything to say to her.

Our adventure is over. Winter this year is dead like the tomb. Perhaps when we die, perhaps death alone will give us the key and the sequel and the end of this lost adventure.

Seurel I used to ask you in former days to think of me. Now however it would be better to forget me. It would be better to forget everything.

....

....

....

A.M.

And this was a new Winter, as dead as the last one had been alive with a mysterious life: the church-square without the actors; the school-yard deserted by the boys at four o'clock...the classroom where I studied alone and without pleasure...In February for the first time of the Winter snow fell, completely enveloping our adventure stories of the previous year, destroying all tracks, effacing the last traces. And I was forced as Meaulnes had asked me to in his letter, to forget everything.

Part III

1.   The Bathing

To smoke a cigarette, to put sugar water on the hair to make it curl, to kiss the girls from the Supplementary School in the roads, and to call "Hi Cornet!" from behind a hedge to tease a passing nun, these were the pleasures of the lads of the countryside. But the bad habits of twenty-one years are easily reformed, and such boys can very often turn into perfectly respectable young men. The case is more serious when the comedian in question is already old and faded. When he occupies himself with coarse stories about the women of the neighbourhood, when he tells countless silly stories about Gilberte Poquelin, to make others laugh…well maybe even then the case is not hopeless…

This was the case with Jasmin Delouche. He continued, I do not know why but certainly not with a desire to pass his examinations, to take the Superior Diploma Course which everyone wished he would abandon. In between he learnt the trade of plasterer with his Uncle Dumas. And soon Jasmin Delouche, with Boujardon, and another very nice boy, the son of the Deputy Mayor, called Denis, were the only senior students with whom I liked to associate, because they belonged to "Meaulnes' time".

Besides, Delouche himself had a very sincere desire to be my friend. For to tell the truth he who had been Meaulnes' enemy had himself wanted to be the big Meaulnes of the school; and at the least he regretted that he had not been his lieutenant. Less coarse than Boujardon he had felt I think all that Meaulnes had brought into our life, all that was extraordinary in him. And often I would hear him repeat,

"How well big Meaulnes used to say…"or again: "Ah! Big Meaulnes used to say…"

Apart from Jasmin being more of the man than we were, this elderly boy shared with us amusing treasures in order to establish his superiority. There was a mongrel dog with long white hair which responded to the irritating name of Becali. It would bring back stones which had been thrown a long way for it but didn't have the aptitude for any other sport. There was an old bicycle bought second-hand which Jasmin made me ride, but on which he preferred to exercise the girls of the district. And above all there was a blind white donkey which could be attached to vehicles.

It was Dumas' donkey, but he lent it to Jasmin when he went to bathe in the River Cher in the Summer. On that occasion his mother would give us a bottle of lemonade which we put under the seat amongst the dry bathing-trunks. And eight to ten of the senior students would set off accompanied by M. Seurel, some on foot, others packed into the donkey-cart which we left at Grand'Fons Farm where the path to the Cher became too furrowed.

I have special reason to remember every detail of one of these trips when Jasmin's donkey drove ahead with our bathing trunks, our bags, the lemonade and M. Seurel, while we followed on foot. It was August. We had just passed the examinations. Delivered from this anxiety it seemed to us as if the whole Summer all happiness belonged to us, and we walked along the road singing without knowing why at the beginning of a beautiful Thursday afternoon.

There was as we went along only one shadow on this innocent scene. We saw walking ahead of us Gilberte Poquelin. She had a nipped-in waist, a medium-length skirt, high-heeled shoes, and the sweet impudent air of a mischievous child who was growing into a young girl. She left the road and took a more winding path in order to look for milk probably. Young Coffin immediately suggested to Jasmin that we follow her.

"It would not be the first time that I have kissed her," said the other.

And he began to recount ribald stories about her and her friends, and the whole party bragged as they went along, leaving M. Seurel to continue ahead on the road in the donkey-cart. Once on the path the party began to separate. Delouche himself did not seem anxious to approach her in front of us, and as she disappeared he did not attempt to go within fifty metres of her. There were several cock and hen cries, and little wolf whistles, and then we abandoned the pursuit and returned to the road rather embarrassed. We had to run along the road in the full heat of the sun. We did not sing any more.

We undressed and dressed in the bare willow-trees which bordered the Cher. The willow trees sheltered us from view but not from the sun. With our feet in the sand and dry earth we could think only of widow Delouche's bottle of lemonade which was being kept cool in the Grand'Fons spring, a spring which rose from the depths of the River Cher itself. There were always blue-green grasses at the bottom and little creatures like wood-lice, but the water was so clear and transparent that the fishermen did not hesitate to kneel down with their hands on either side to drink from it.

Alas! It was a day like all the others...but when we were dressed and seated in a circle, cross-legged like tailors to share the refreshing lemonade which was divided into two large glasses and had asked M. Seurel to take his share, there remained hardly more than a little froth for each of us to tantalise the throat and aggravate the thirst. So in turn we went to the spring which we had earlier despised and slowly lowered our faces to the surface of the pure water. But we were unused to the habits of the country people. Many like me could not manage to quench their thirst, some because they did not like the water, others because they had tightened their throats for fear of swallowing a wood-louse. Others again, deceived by the great transparency of the water and not knowing how to calculate the distance plunged in part of their faces, and inhaled water sharply through their noses so that it seemed to burn them, and others yet again for all these reasons at once...It didn't matter! It seemed to us on the arid banks of the Cher that all earthly refreshment reposed in this place. And even now, at the single word, fountain, wherever I hear it, it is of that place that I think for a long time.

We returned at dusk, carefree at first, as when we set out. The Grand'Fons path which climbed towards the road was a stream in Winter, and in Summer an impossible gully full of holes and thick roots concealed in the dark between the great hedges of trees. A party of bathers was playing these. Jasmin and several comrades and I, along with M. Seurel, took a gentle sandy path parallel to that one which bordered the neighbouring land. We heard the talk and laughter of others close by below us, invisiblwe in the dark while Delouche narrated his manly exploits...Above the trees of the tall hedge we could see insects of the evening against the clear sky and moving in the lacy pattern of the foliage. Sometimes he would brush one away sharply when its buzzing annoyed him. How fine was that calm Summer evening!...to return without hope but without desire from a simple outing in the country...It was again Jasmin who unintentionally disturbed this peace...

As we arrived at the top of the slope where there were two large stones which seemed to have belonged to some big chateau he began to talk of Chateaux he had visited and especially about a manor-house which was partially deserted in the district of Vieux-Nancay: the Sablonnieres manor. With his Allier accent which rounded off certain words and cut short others in a vain affectation, he told us about having seen several years before in the ruined chapel of that old property a tomb-stone which was engraved with the words:

"Here lies the chevalier Galoiis,

Faithful to his God, to his King, and his lover."

"Ha! Bah!" said M. Seurel with a slow shrug of the shoulders, a little embarrassed by the tone of the conversation, but desiring nevertheless that we should talk like men.

Then Jasmin continued to describe the chateau as if he had spent his life there.

Several times, on returning to Vieux-Nancay, Dumas and he had been intrigued by an old grey tower which could be seen above the fir-trees. There was there in the middle of the wood a whole maze of ruined buildings which in the absence of the owners one could visit. Once one of the guards of the place to whom they had given a lift in their carriage, had taken them to the strange Domaine. But since that time it had all been demolished; it was said that all that remained was the farm and a small house. The inhabitants were always the same, an old retired officer, half ruined, and his daughter.

He talked...and talked...I listened attentively without thinking about it that this concerned something well-known to me, when suddenly, quite simply, as extraordinary things do occur, Jasmin turned to me and touched my arm, struck by an idea which had not occurred to him before;

"You know," he said, "I think it was there that Meaulnes — you know big Meaulnes? – must have gone."

121

"Of course," he added, when I did not reply, "and I remember the guard talked about the son of the house who was an eccentric and given to extraordinary ideas"...

I listened no more, persuaded from the beginning that he had guessed correctly and that before me, far from Meaulnes, far from all hope, as neatly and easily as a familiar road, the path to the nameless Domaine had been disclosed.

2.   At Florentin's

As I had once been a sad, introverted and dreary child, so I now became resolute, and as we say at home "decided" when I felt that the outcome of this grave adventure depended on me.

It was, I well believe, from that evening that my knee ceased permanently to trouble me.

At Vieux-Nancay, which was in the district of the Sablonnieres manor, there lived the whole family of M. Seurel, and in particular my Uncle Florentin. He was a business-man with whom we sometimes spent the end of September. Freed from examinations I did not want to wait to obtain permission to go immediately to visit my uncle. But I decided not to make this known to Meaulnes until I was certain of being able to give him good news. What good would it be to tear him away from his despair only to plunge him in again later, perhaps even deeper?

For a long time Vieux-Nancay had been the place I liked best in the world. The end-of-the-holidays place where we went rarely and only then when there was a carriage available to hire to drive us there. There had once been some sort of quarrel with the branch of the family which lived there and that no doubt was why Millie needed so much persuading every time to get into the carriage. But I did not bother with such bickering!...And as soon as we arrived I would be lost amongst uncles and cousins in a life full of amusing occupations and delightful pleasures.

We would alight at the house of my Uncle Florentin and Aunt Julie. They had a son my age, my cousin Firman, and eight daughters, of whom the two elder, Marie-Louise and Charlotte, must have been seventeen and fifteen. They kept a big shop at one of the entrances to the town of Sologne, in front of the church. It was a general store where all the leading towns-people got their provisions, isolated as they were in a remote region, thirty kilometres from any station.

This shop with its' grocery counter, and printed cotton counter, looked out through many windows on to the road, and through glass doors on to the great church square. But strange to say, common enough as it was in that poor locality, the beaten earth served throughout the shop as a floor.

Behind there were six rooms, each full of one of the items of merchandise: the hat room, the garden-produce room, the lamp room...what else? It seemed to me as a child and made my way through the maze of bazaar items that I had no hope of ever seeing all the marvels. And even at that time I would feel there was no true holiday except those spent in that place.

The family lived in a large kitchen, the door of which opened into the shop. In that kitchen at the end of September there would be blazing fires where hunters and poachers who came early morning to sell game to Florentin would be served something to drink while the younger girls, already up, would run and shout, putting perfume on each other's smooth hair. On the walls old photographs, old yellowed school-groups showed my father, difficult to distinguish in his school uniform amongst the other pupils of his school...

It was there where we spent our mornings, and also in the yard where Florentin grew dahlias and raised guinea-fowl, or we roasted coffee seated on boxes of soap. Or we would open boxes full of all sorts of carefully-wrapped objects whose names we did not always know...

The whole day the shop was invaded by peasants or by coachmen from the neighbouring chateaux. Carts coming in from the depths of the countryside would halt in front of the glass door, dripping in the September mist. And from the kitchen we would listen to what the peasants said, curious to hear all their stories...

But in the evening, after eight o'clock, when, carrying lanterns, we took hay to the horses whose hides smoked in the stable – the whole shop belonged to us!

Marie-Louise who was the oldest of my cousins but one of the smallest, managed to fold up and arrange the piles of cloth in the shop, and then invited up to come and amuse her. Firman and I with all the girls would raid the big shop by the light from the inn, turning coffee-mills, and jumping on to the counters, and sometimes, because the beaten-earth floor invited dancing, Firman would search in the attics for some old trombone covered with vert-de-gris...

I still blush at the thought that in previous years Mlle de Galais could have come at that time and surprised us in the middle of these childish games…But it was little before nightfall one evening of that August while I was talking quietly with Marie-Louise and Firman, that I saw her for the first time…

Since the evening of my arrival in Viieux-Nancay, I had been asking my Uncle Florentin about the manor of Sablonnieres.

"It is no longer a manor." He said. "Everything has been sold and the people who bought it are hunters. So they have demolished the old buildings to enlarge the hunting area; the great yard is now a wilderness of heather and gorse. The former owners have kept only a small bungalow and the farm. You will have plenty of opportunity to see Mlle de Galais here; she comes herself to get their provisions, sometimes on horse-back, sometimes in the carriage, but always the same old horse, Belisaire…it's a strange equipage!"

I was so disturbed that I did not know how to put my questions to the best advantage.

"They used to be rich though?"

"Yes. M. de Galais used to give parties to entertain his son, a strange boy full of extraordinary ideas. To keep him occupied they did whatever they could. They brought in girls and boys from Paris even!…

"The Sablonnieres was all in ruins, Mme de Galais near her end, but they still searched for ways to amuse him and fulfill all his fantasies. It was last Winter – no the Winter before, that they had their grandest Fete in fancy dress. They had invited some guests from Paris and some from the countryside. They had hired huge quantities of fancy-dress costumes, games, horses, boats. All to amuse Frantz de Galais. It was said he was going to be married and all this was to entertain the fiancés. But he was much too young. Then suddenly everything was destroyed. He ran away and has not been seen since. The chatelaine died. Mlle de Galais was left alone with her father, the old sea-captain."

"Isn't she married?" I asked at last.

"No," he said, "I never heard mention of that. Are you a suitor then?"

Taken aback, I confessed to him as briefly and discreetly as possible, that my best friend, Augustin Meaulnes, would perhaps be one."

"Ah!" said Florentin, smiling, "If he doesn't want a fortune it is a good match...Would he like to speak to M. de Galais? He sometimes comes as far as this shop looking for hunting shot. I always make him sample my old brandy."

But I asked him quickly to do nothing, but wait. And I would hasten to inform Meaulnes. Such an accumulation of happy chances disquieted me a little. And this disquiet persuaded me to tell Meaulnes nothing until I had at last seen the young girl.

I did not wait long. The next day, shortly before dinner as it was getting dark, a fresh mist more like September than August descended with the night. Firman and I, seeing the shop to be empty of customers for a moment, came in to see Marie-Louise and Charlotte. I had confided to them the secret which had brought me to Vieux-Nancay at this early date. Leaning on the counter or seated on it with our hands flat on the polished wood, we were confiding to each other all that we knew of the mysterious young girl – and that amounted to very little – when the sound of wheels made us turn our heads.

"Here she is, this is she," they said in low voices.

After a few minutes in front of the glass door stopped the strange equipage. It was an old farm vehicle with rounded panels and little moulded seats unlike anything we ever saw in that region. It had an old white horse which seemed to want only to graze on the grass along the road, and on the seat – I say in the simplicity of my heart knowing full well what I say – there was the most beautiful girl that there had perhaps ever been in the world.

Never had I seen such grace united with such gravity. Her dress fitted so closely into a waist so narrow that she seemed fragile. A great chestnut-coloured cloak which she took off as she entered had been thrown round her shoulders. She was the most serious of girls, the frailest of women. The weight of blond hair seemed too heavy for her forehead and delicate face. On her pure complexion there were two freckles...I noticed only one defect in so much beauty: in moments of distress, or discouragement, or only of deep reflection, the purity of her skin would be marbled slowly with pink, as happens in certain grave illnesses which have not been discovered. Then all the admiration in those looking at her would be replaced by a kind of pity, all the more heart-rending in that she observed it.

This at least is what I noticed as she descended slowly from the carriage, and at last Marie-Louise presented me to her and drew me easily into conversation with her.

We offered her a polished chair and she sat leaning on the counter while we remained standing. She seemed to know and love the shop. My Aunt Julie, informed immediately, arrived in her white bonnet, and while she talked sagely, her hands clasped across her stomach and her head shaking gently, in the style of country business-women, delayed the moment, causing me to tremble a little, when the conversation would include me...

It was very simple.

"So," said Mlle de Galais, "you will soon be a teacher?"

Over our heads my Aunt lit the porcelain lamp which gave out a feeble light in the shop. I saw the sweet childish face of the girl, her eyes blue and innocent and I was all the more surprised by the clarity and seriousness of her voice. When she stopped speaking her eyes looked elsewhere, unmoving as she waited for the reply, and she would bite the corner of her lip.

"I would also like to teach," she said, "if M. de Galais would allow it. I would teach little boys as your mother does"...

And she smiled, as she showed me that my cousins had spoken of me.

"The villagers," she continued, "are always polite to me, sweet and obliging, and I love them a lot. But what merit do I have in loving them?"...

"When they are with their teacher they are mischievous and mean, are they not? There are endless stories of lost pens, exercise-books which are too expensive, or of children who won't learn...Well I would struggle with them, and they would love me all the same. That would be much more difficult"....

And, without smiling, she resumed her dreamy childish pose, her blue eyes immobile.

We were all three embarrassed by the ease with which she spoke on these delicate subjects, on what is secret and subtle and of which one does not speak except in books. There was a moment of silence, and then slowly the discussion continued...

"And then I would teach the boys to be wise, with a wisdom which I know. I would not give them the desire to rub around the world, as you will no doubt M. Seurel, when you are a teacher. I would teach them to find happiness in what is close to them and which may not seem to be happiness"...

Marie-Louise and Firman were as embarrassed as I was. We said nothing. She sensed our awkwardness and stopped, biting her lip, and lowering her head. And then she smiled as if in mockery:

"And so," she said, "perhaps there is some big young man, who foolishly searches for me at the ends of the earth while I am here in Mme Florentin's shop under this lamp, while my old horse waits at the door. If this young man saw me he would not want to believe it probably?"...

Seeing her smile I was seized with audacity, and felt it was time to speak. So, laughing also, I said,

"And perhaps I know this big foolish young man?"

She looked at me eagerly.

At that moment the doorbell rang and two women came in with baskets;

"Come into the dining-room where you will be in peace," said my Aunt pushing open the kitchen door.

And as Mlle de Galais was about to refuse and leave immediately my Aunt said,

"M. de Galais is here and is talking to Florentin by the fire."

There was always, even in August, an eternal fir log fire burning and crackling in the big kitchen. In there also a porcelain lamp had been lit, and seated next to Florentin in front of two glasses of brandy was a sweet-faces old man. The skin of his face was wrinkled and furrowed, and he sat silently most of the time as if weighed down with age and memories.

Florentin greeted us.

"Francois!" he cried in the loud voice of a commercial traveler as if a river and several hectares of land stood between us. "I have just organized an afternoon's picnic party on the banks of the River Cher for next Thursday. Some people will hunt, others will dance, others will bathe!...Mademoiselle, you will come on horseback; that is agreed with M. de Galais. I have arranged everything"...

"And Francois!" he added as if he had only just thought of it, "You can bring your friend M. Meaulnes ...his name is Meaulnes isn't it?"

Mlle de Galais rose, suddenly very pale. And at that moment I remembered that on one occasion in the strange manor beside the pond , Meaulnes had given her his name...

When she took my hand to leave there was between us, clearer than if we had spoken many words, a secret understanding which only death could break and a friendship deeper than a great love.

...At four o'clock the next morning Firman knocked at the door of the little bedroom where I stayed in the poultry-yard. It was still dark and I had difficulty finding my things on the table cluttered with copper chandeliers and perfectly new statues of saints chosen from the shop to furnish my room the night of my arrival. In the yard I could hear Firman pumping my bicycle tyres, and in the kitchen my Aunt blowing the fire. I would lunch first at Sainte-Agathe to explain my extended absence, and continuing my route I would arrive at Ferte-d'Angillon at the house of my friend Augustin Meaulnes.

3. An Apparition

I had never ridden far on a bicycle. This was my first time. But a long time ago Jasmin had taught me in spite of my knee to get on. If even for a normal young man a bicycle is an enjoyable instrument how must it seem to a poor boy like me who until recently had trailed one leg miserably and was bathed in sweat after four kilometers!....To descend from the tops of hills and disappear into the hollows of the countryside; to experience as if on wings the distances of the road which spread out and blossomed as you approached; to pass through a village in the space of an instant and carry it all away in the glance of an eye....only in dreams had I known up till then such a journey, as pleasurable as it was easy. Even the hills found me full of zeal. For this was, it should be said, the road through Meaulnes' countryside, which I was drinking in...

"A little before you enter the town," Meaulnes had once told me while describing his village, "you see a big paddle-wheel turned by the wind..."He did not know what purpose it served, or maybe he pretended not to know in order to pique my curiosity the more.

It was almost towards the end of that fine August day that I saw, turning in the wind in a huge field, the great wheel which must raise water for a neighbouring farm. Beyond the poplars bordering the field the first suburbs could already be seen. As I followed the long detour which the road took to cross a stream the scenery expanded and unfolded around me. Arriving at the bridge I discovered at last the main road to the village.

Cows were passing by hidden in the reeds of the field, and I could hear their bells as I got off the bicycle. With both hands on the handle-bar I surveyed the land where I was about to bring such serious news. Where one entered by crossing the little wooden bridge the houses stood above a ditch along the road-side, like so many ships with their sails furled, moored in the calm of the evening. It was the hour when in each kitchen the fire was being lit.

Then fear, and I don't know what obscure regret for coming to trouble such peace, began to sap away my courage. Just at that moment, to aggravate my sudden weakness, I remembered that my Aunt Moinel lived there in the small square of Ferte-d'Angillon.

She was one of my great-aunts. All her children were dead, and the last of all, Ernest, I had known well. He was a big boy and going to be a teacher. My Great-Uncle Moinel, an elderly clerk of court followed closely after him. And my Aunt was left all alone in her strange little house, where the carpets were samples of cloth stitched together. The table-cloths consisted of pictures of cocks, hens and cats cut out of paper. The walls were covered with old diplomas, portraits of people who had died, and lo9ckets with curls from dead horses.

With so much sorrow and mourning she combined eccentricity with good humour. When I had found the little square where she lived I called loudly to her through the open door, and I heard her voice from the last of three rooms which stood in a line, giving a little shrill cry:

"What! Good gracious!"

She upset her coffee into the fire. How could she be making coffee at that hour?...And she appeared... Her back was very bent, and she wore a cape with a sort of hood or cap on the top of her head above an immense and bumpy forehead like those of Mongolian or Hottentot women. And she laughed with little cries, showing her fine teeth.

But while I embraced her she took my hand from behind her back clumsily and hastily. With quite un-necessary mystery since we were alone she slipped into it a coin at which I dared not look and which must be a franc...Then when I pretended to demand explanations and thank her, she gave me a push, crying,

"Go along then! Ha! I know how it is."

She had always been poor, always borrowing, always spending.

"I have always been foolish, and always unhappy," she said without bitterness but in her falsetto voice.

Persuaded that money preoccupied me as it did her, the good woman did not wait till I had caught my breath before hiding in my hand her small economies of the day. And afterwards it was always thus that she welcomed me.

Dinner was just as strange – at once sad and bizarre – as the reception. There was always a candle within reach of her hand. Sometimes she would take it away, leaving me in the dark, other times leave it on the table covered with plates and chipped or cracked vases.

"That one," she said, "the Prussians broke the handles of in 1870 because they could not take it away."

I remembered only then, seeing the big vase again with its' tragic story, that we had dined and slept here once before. My father brought me in L' Yonne to a specialist who was to cure my knee. We had to catch an express which came through before dawn...I remembered that sad dinner of long ago, and all the stories told by the old clerk of court as he leant in front of his bottle of rose-coloured liquid.

And I remembered also my terrors...After dinner, sitting in front of the fire, my Great-Aunt had taken my Father aside to tell him a story about ghosts:

"I came back...Ah! My poor Louis, what's this that I see, a little grey woman..."She was known for having her head stuffed with these terrifying nonsenses.

And that evening after dinner, when tired from the bicycling, I was put in a big room with a checked night-shirt which had belonged to my Uncle Moinel, she came to sit at my bedside and began to tell me in her most mysterious and high-pitched tones,

"My poor Francois, I must tell you something I have never told anyone..."

I thought:

"This is good, here I am to be terrorised for the whole night, just like ten years ago!"...

And I listened. She shook her head, looking straight ahead of her as if she was telling the story to herself:

"I returned from the Fete with Moinel. It was the first marriage we both attended after the death of our poor Ernest, and there I met my sister Adele whom I had not met for four years! An old friend of Moinel's who was very rich had invited him to the wedding of his son at the Sablonnieres manor. We hired a carriage. It cost us a lot. We were returning along the road about seven o'clock in the morning in mid-Winter. The sun came up. There was absolutely no-one about. What do I see suddenly on the road in front of us? A young man, a small man standing still, beautiful as the day, who didn't move and watched us coming. As we approached we could see his pretty face, so white, so pretty, that I was afraid!...

I took Moinel's arm, I trembled like a leaf; I thought it was the good God...I said to him:

"Look! There's a ghost!"

He replied in a low voice, furious,

"I can see him very well! Be quiet chatterbox...."

"He did not know what to do; when the horse stopped...Close to, we saw his face was very pale and his forehead sweating. He wore a grimy beret and long trousers. We heard his sweet voice, saying,

"-I am not a man, I am a girl. I am running away and I can't go any further. Would you give me a lift in your carriage please, Sir and Madame?"

"We made her climb in straight away. Hardly had she sat down than she lost consciousness. And can you guess who she was? She was the fiancée of the young man of the Sablonnieres, Frantz de Galais, to whose marriage we had been invited!"

"But there had been no marriage because the fiancée ran away!" I said.

"No," she said, a little abashed, "there had been no marriage because the poor silly girl's head was full of a thousand foolish ideas which she explained to us. She was one of the daughters of a poor weaver. She was persuaded that so much happiness was impossible; that the young man was too young for her; that all the marvels he had described were imaginary, and when finally Frantz came to fetch her Valentine took fright. He walked with her and her sister in the Archbishop's garden in Bourges in spite of the cold and the strong wind. The young man out of delicacy no doubt because he loved the younger sister, paid a lot of attention to the older girl. Then the silly girl began to imagine I don't know what. She said she was going to get a scarf from the house. And when she got there she dressed in these men's clothes so as not to be followed, and set off on foot on the road to Paris.

"Her fiancé received a letter from her in which she said she was going to re-join a man she loved. And that was not true..............

"'I am happier in my sacrifice,' she told me, 'than I would be as his wife.' Yes, little imbecile, but meanwhile he had no idea at all of marrying her sister. He shot himself. They saw the blood in the wood but never found his body."

"And what did you do with the unhappy girl?"

"We made her drink something first. And when we got home we gave her something to eat and she slept by the fire. She stayed with us most of the Winter. All day when the weather was bright she tailored and sewed garments, fixed hats, and cleaned the house industriously. It was she who did all this tapestry work you can see. And since she was here, swallows have been nesting outside. But, in the evening, at nightfall, when her work was finished she would always find some pretext for going into the yard, into the garden, or just outside the door, even when there was a hard frost. And we would discover her standing there weeping with all her heart.

"'Well, what's the matter now? Tell me.'

'Nothing Madame Moinel.'

"And she would come inside. The neighbours would say,

"You have found a very good pretty little servant Mme Moinel."

" In spite of our supplications she wanted to continue on her way to Paris in March. I gave her frocks which she re-made. Moinel got her ticket at the station and gave her a little money. She hasn't forgotten us. She is a dress-maker in Paris near Notre-Dame. She still writes to know if we have news of Sablonnieres. On one occasion I told her, to free her from these preoccupations, that the manor is sold, and destroyed, the young man disappeared for ever, and the daughter married. All that must be true I think. Since then Valentin writes much less often..."

This was not a story of ghosts my Aunt Moinel was recounting in the little strident voice so well suited for them. I was meanwhile in an agony of discomfort. Had we not sworn to Frantz the actor to serve him like brothers and here an opportunity had been offered to me..............

Or was this the moment to spoil the joy I was bringing to Meaulnes the following morning by telling him what I had just learnt? What was the use of thrusting him into a totally impossible enterprise" We had more or less the address of the girl, but where to look for the actor who was running all over the world?....Leave the fools with the fools, I thought. Delouche and Boujardon had not been wrong. What harm Frantz the romantic had done to us! And I decided to say nothing until I had seen Augustin Meaulnes married to Mlle de Galais.

This resolution taken, there still remained a sense of foreboding – an absurd impression which I dismissed quickly.

The candle was nearly at an end; a mosquito vibrated; but my Aunt Moinel, her head bent under her velvet hood which she did not take off even to sleep, her elbows resting on her knees, took up her story again...Now and then she would raise her head suddenly to see my reactions, or perhaps to see if I was sleeping. In the end, slyly, my head on my pillow, I closed my eyes and pretended to doze off.

"Oh, I see, you're asleep....," she said in a voice a little muffled and disappointed.

I took pity on her and protested:

"No, not at all, Aunt, I promise you..."

"Yes," she said, "and in any case I can understand that all that will hardly interest you. I'm talking about people you do not know..."

And this time, like a coward, I did not reply.

4.   The Great News

The next morning when I reached the main road it was fine holiday weather, and so calm, and in the town the sounds were so peaceful and familiar, that I regained all the joyful confidence of a bearer of good news...

Augustin and his mother lived in an ancient school-house. On the death of his father who had been retired a long time and whom an inheritance had made wealthy, Meaules had wanted to buy the school where the elderly teacher had taught for twenty years and where he himself had learnt to read. Not that it had a pleasant appearance: it was a huge square house, having been earlier a town-hall. The windows on the ground-floor which looked out on to the road were so high no-one ever looked out of them, and the back yard, where no tree ever grew and whose tall shed barred the view to the countryside, was the most barren and desolate of abandoned school-yards I ever saw.

In the complicated passage into which four doors opened, I found Meaulnes' mother bringing in a large bundle of clothes from the garden which must have been put to dry very early that holiday morning. Her grey hair was half undone and some locks fell across her face. Her regular features under the hair were swollen with fatigue as if after a sleepless night and her head was bowed sadly like one in a dream.

But suddenly seeing me and recognizing me she smiled:

"You have arrived just in time," she said. "I am bringing in the clothes I was drying for Meaulnes' departure. I have spent the night sorting out his things and getting everything ready for him. The train leaves at five o'clock, but we will manage to be ready."...

She showed so much assurance one would have t she had made this decision herself. But probably she did not even know where Meaulnes had to go.

"Go upstairs," she said. "You will find him in the town-hall writing."

Hastily I climbed the stairs and opened the door on the right on which the word "Town-Hall" was still inscribed and found myself in a large room with four windows, two looking on to the town, two on to the countryside. The walls were decorated with yellowed portraits of Presidents Grevy and Carnot. On a long platform which took up one end of the room, there were still in front of a table covered with a green cloth the municipal councillors' chairs. In the middle, seated on an old armchair which used to belong to the mayor, Meaulnes was writing, dipping his pen into an inkwell of old-fashioned earthenware shaped like a heart. To this place which seemed suited to some villager with private means, Meaulnes retired during the long holidays when he was not travelling...

He rose as soon as he recognised me but not with the enthusiasm I had expected:

"Seurel!" was all he said in profound astonishment.

It was the same large boy with the bony face and shaved head. An untrained moustache was beginning to hang over his lips. There was the same steadfast expression...But over the ardour of past years there seemed to be something like a veil of mist which moment by moment his great passion of former times dispersed...

He seemed to be agitated at the sight of me. In one bound I had mounted the platform. But, strange to say, he did not think of offering me his hand. He turned towards me with his hands behind his back leaning on the table, dumb-founded and embarrassed. Already he looked at me without seeing me, absorbed in thinking what to say to me. As in former times and as always he was slow to begin to speak. Like solitary people, and hunters or adventurers, he had taken a decision without considering the words he would need to explain himself. And only as I stood before him did he start to search painfully for the necessary words.

Meanwhile I told him gaily how I had come, where I had passed the night, and that I had been surprised to find Mme Meaulnes preparing for her son's departure.

"Ah! She told you?"... he asked.

"Yes. It isn't I hope for as long journey?"

"Yes. A very long journey."

Disconcerted for a moment, and fearing that with one word I might reduce this decision, which I could not understand, to nothing, I dare say no more and did not know how to begin my mission.

But he himself spoke in the end, as if wishing to justify himself.

"Seurel," he said, "you know what my strange adventure in Sainte-Agathe was for me. It was my reason for living and for having hope. That hope is lost. What is to become of me?....How can I live like the rest of the world!

I tried to live in Paris when I saw that everything was finished, and there was no more point in even trying to look for the lost Domain...But a man who has once leapt into Paradise - how can he ever afterwards accept the life of the rest of the world? What is happiness to others appears to me as a joke. And then when I decided one day, sincerely and deliberately, to do like others I heaped up remorse which will last a long time...."

Seated on a chair on the platform, my head lowered, listening to him without looking at him, I did not know what to make of this obscure explanation.

"Anyway," I said, "explain why this long journey? Have you some fault to expiate? Some promise to keep?

"Well yes," he replied, "you remember the promise I made to Frantz?

"Ah." I said reassured, "It's just a question of that?"

"Of that, and also perhaps a fault to expiate. Both together at the same time..."

There followed a moment of silence during which I decided to begin my story, and was preparing my words.....

"I believe there is only one explanation," he said at last. "Certainly I would have liked to have seen Mlle de Galais one more time...only seen her...But I believe now that when I discovered the nameless Domain I was elevated to a height, to a degree of perfection and purity, which I can never attain again. Only in death perhaps, as I wrote to you once, will I find again the beauty of that time…"

His tone was suddenly full of a strange animation as he approached me:

"But listen Seurel. This new scheme and this long journey, this fault which I committed and have to make good, it is still in a sense my old adventure which I am pursuing...."

For a moment he paused, trying painfully to assemble his memories. I had missed my earlier opportunity. I did not want for anything in the world to lose this. This time I spoke – too fast, for I regretted bitterly later not having waited for his confession.

I spoke then the words which I had prepared earlier but which were no longer appropriate. I said without any movement, hardly raising my head,

"And if I were to tell you that all hope is not lost?".....

He looked at me then, turning his eyes suddenly towards me, his face red as I had never seen anyone blush, a rush of blood which caused his temples to throb.

"What are you trying to say?" he asked at last in muffled words.

Then I told him clearly all that I knew, what I had done, and how. With everything now changed, it seemed almost as if it was Yvonne de Galais who had sent me to him.

He was now frighteningly pale.

During this recital to which he had listened in silence, his head thrown back a little in the attitude of someone who has been surprised and does not know how to defend himself, whether to hide or whether to flee, he interrupted me only once I remember. I told him in passing that the Sablonnieres had been demolished and that the Domain of former times no longer existed.

"Ah," he said, "you see," (as if he sought an occasion to justify his conduct and the despair in which he was engulfed) "you see, there is nothing left..."

Finally, believing that the convenience of it all would remove all his difficulties, I told him about the picnic party which had been organized by my Uncle Florentin. That Mlle de Galais was to arrive there on horse-back and that he himself was invited.......But he appeared to be completely bewildered and continued to say nothing.

"You must cancel your journey immediately," I said impatiently. "Come along. We'll tell your Mother..."

And as we both went downstairs,

"This picnic party?" he asked hesitantly, "I really have to be there?"

"But of course," I replied. "There's no question about that."

He looked like someone who had been pushed behind the shoulders. Downstairs Augustin told Mme Meaulnes that I would lunch and dine and sleep with them, and that next day he would also hire a bicycle to follow me to Vieux-Nancy.

"Ah, very good," she said, nodding her head as if these tidings had confirmed her own expectations.

I sat in the small dining-room under illustrated calendars, ornamental daggers, and Sudanese water-skins which a brother of M. Meaulnes who had been in the navy had brought back from his long voyages.

Augustin left me there for a moment before the meal, and in the adjoining room where his mother had packed the bags I heard him telling her quietly not to unpack his luggage as the journey was only delayed.

5. The Picnic Party

I had difficulty following Augustin on the road to Vieux-Nancay. He went like a racing cyclist and did not get off on the slopes. His inexplicable hesitation of the day before had been succeeded by a fever, an agitation, a desire to get there as quickly as possible, which frightened me a little. At my Uncle's house he showed the same impatience. He appeared incapable of taking any interest in anything until we were installed in the carriage at about ten o'clock the next morning and ready to leave for the banks of the river.

It was the end of August and the Summer. Already the empty shells of the yellow chestnuts were beginning to litter the white roads. The journey was not long. The Aubiers' farm near to the Cher where we were going was hardly two kilometers beyond the Sablonnieres. From time to time we met other guests in their vehicles and young people on horse-back which Florentin had commandeered audaciously in the name of M. de Galais. It was inevitable that as once before, rich and poor, chatelains and peasants, were mixed together. It was thus that we saw Jasmin Delouche arriving on his bicycle. Thanks to the guard, Baladier, he had met my Uncle some time earlier.

"And there," said Meaulnes on seeing him, "is the one who had the key to everything, while we were searching as far as Paris. It is enough to make one despair!"

Every time he looked at Jasmin his rancor increased, while he on the contrary imagined he had the right to our comradeship. He escorted our carriage closely to the end. It was evident that he had tried to dress for the occasion but without much success. The sides of his threadbare jacket hung against the mudguard of his bicycle........

In spite of the effort he made to be friendly his little old man's appearance could not possibly please. He filled me with a vague sense of pity. But whom would I not have pitied on that journey?

I never remember that pleasure party without an obscure regret like a suffocation. I had looked forward to that day with so much joy!

Everything seemed to be perfectly arranged for our happiness. And we had so little!......

Yet the banks of the Cher were so beautiful! By the river where we stopped the hillside ended in a gentle slope, and the land was divided into little green fields, separated by fences like so many tiny gardens. On the other side of the river the banks formed grey hills which were rocky and sharp, and on the more distant hills one could see among the fir trees little romantic-looking chateaux with turrets. In the distance from time to time we could hear the barking of a pack of hounds from the Preveranges chateau.

We had reached that place through a maze of little paths, sometimes scattered with white pebbles, sometimes sandy, which when they reached their living sources at the banks of the river were transformed into streams. Along the way the branches of prickly currant bushes caught at our sleeves. Sometimes we were plunged into the fresh darkness of the vegetation, and then the hedges would be interrupted and we were bathed in the clear light of the whole valley. In the distance, as we approached, a man who was leaning on some rocks on the opposite bank, pulled on his fishing line with a leisurely gesture. How good it all was, my God!

We settled ourselves on a lawn in a secluded spot surrounded by birch trees. It was a large mown lawn where there seemed to be space for endless games.

The carriages were unharnessed and the horses taken to the Aubiers' farm. We began to unpack the provisions in the wood, and to set up little collapsible tables, which my Uncle had brought, on the grass.

It was necessary then for willing people to go to the end of the nearby main road to watch for the last arrivals and show them where we were. I offered immediately and Meaulnes followed, and we went to stand near the suspension bridge at the crossroads of several roads including the path which came from the Sablonnieres.

Walking to and fro, talking of the past, and trying however unsuccessfully to distract our minds, we waited. A carriage arrived from Vieux-Nancy full of unknown peasants with a large beribboned girl. Then nothing. Oh yes, there were three children in a donkey-cart, the children of the old gardener of the Sablonnieres

"I seem to recognise them," said Meaulnes, "These are the ones who took me by the hand once, the first evening of the fete, and took me into dinner..."

But at that moment the donkey decided not to walk, and the children got down to poke him, pull him, and hit him as hard as they could. So Meaulnes, disappointed, pretended to be mistaken.......

I asked them if on the way they had met M. and Mlle de Galais. One replied that he did not know, the other, "I think so Monsieur." And we were no wiser. In the end they went down towards the lawn, some pulling the donkey by the bridle, others pushing the cart behind. We resumed our wait. Meaulnes looked fixedly at the bend in the path from the Sablonnieres, watching with a sort of dread for the arrival of the young girl whom he had once searched for so long. A strange almost comic excitement which he had aroused in Jasmin, now engulfed him. From the little slope we had climbed to see further along the path we could see a group of guests on the lawn below before whom Delouche was trying to cut a good figure.

"Look at the orator! Silly fool," Meaulnes said to me. And I replied,

"Let him alone. He does what he can poor boy."

Augustin was not disarmed. Below a hare or a squirrel must have come out of a thicket, and Jasmin, to restore his self-esteem, pretended to run after it.

"Oh good. He's running now," said Meaulnes, as if this audacity surpassed all the others.

And this time I could not help laughing. Meaulnes did too, but it was no more than a shout.

After another quarter of an hour, "Suppose she does not come," he said. I replied,

"But since she promised.... Be more patient."

He began watching again. But at last, incapable of bearing this intolerable wait any longer, he said,

"Listen, I'm going down to the others. I don't know what is against me now, but I sense that if I remain here she will never come, that it is impossible that at the end of this road she will soon make her appearance."

And he went away towards the lawn, leaving me alone. I walked some hundred metres along the road to pass the time. And at the first turning I saw Yvonne de Galais mounted side-saddle on an old white horse which this morning was so lively she was obliged to pull on the reins to prevent it trotting. At the head of the horse, painfully and in silence, walked M.de Galais. There was no doubt that along the path they had had to take it in turns to lead the old horse.

When the young girl saw me alone she smiled, jumped nimbly to the ground, and entrusting the reins to her Father came towards me as I ran.

"I'm glad to find you alone," she said, "for I don't want to show old Belisaire to anyone but you, nor put him with the other horses. First of all he's too ugly and too old; and then I'm always afraid he will be wounded by one of the others. For he is the only one I dare mount, and when he dies I will no longer ride a horse."

In Mlle de Galais, as in Meaulnes, I felt under the charming animation, under the gracious and tranquil appearance, an impatience which was almost anxiety. She was talking faster than usual. In spite of her pink cheeks and cheekbones, there was around her eyes and on her forehead in places, a terrible pallor which betrayed her agitation.

We decided to tether Belisaire to a tree in a little wood near the road. Old M. de Galais, without a word as usual, took the animal from the shafts, and fastened him, a little low it seemed to me. I promised to have hay, oats, and straw sent from the farm soon.......

And Mlle de Galais arrived on the lawn as once before, I imagine, she descended to the bank of the lake when Meaulnes saw her for the first time.

Giving her arm to her Father, and with her left hand holding open the flap of the big light cloak which enveloped her, she advanced towards the guests with an air at once so serious and so childlike. I walked beside her. All the guests scattered, and those playing at a distance stood and assembled to welcome them. There was a brief moment of silence during which each one watched her approach

Meaulnes was amongst a group of young men and there was nothing to distinguish him from his companions except his tall figure: still there were other young men there almost as tall as he. He did nothing which could attract her attention, neither a gesture nor a step forward. I watched him, dressed in grey, immobile, his eyes fixed like all the others on the beautiful girl who was approaching. At last with an unconscious movement he passed his hand in an embarrassed way over his bare head, as if to hide his peasant's shaved hair amongst the well-groomed heads of his companions.

Then the group surrounded Mlle de Galais. The young girls and boys she did not know were presented to her...the turn of my companion was coming and I felt equally as anxious as he could have been. I got ready to make the presentation myself.

But before I could say anything the young girl advanced towards him with surprising gravity and decision:

"I recognize Augustin Meaulnes," she said. And she held out her hand to him.

6.   The Picnic Party (conclusion)

New arrivals approached almost immediately to greet Yvonne de Galais, and the two young people found themselves separated. Unhappily, chance dictated that they were not to be reunited at the same little table for lunch. But Meaulnes seemed to have recovered his confidence and courage. I found myself isolated between Delouche and M. de Galais, but on several occasions I would look at my companion and he would lift his hand in a signal of friendship.

It was towards the end of the afternoon when games, bathing, conversations, and boating on a neighbouring pond were in full swing everywhere that Meaulnes found himself again in the presence of the young girl. We were seated on garden chairs we had brought, chatting with Delouche, when deliberately leaving a group of young people where she seemed to be bored, Mlle de Galais approached us. She asked us, I remember, why we did not go boating on the Aubiers lake like the others.

"We did several rounds this afternoon," I replied, "but it gets monotonous and we were soon bored"

"Well why not go on the river?" she said.

"The currant is too strong. We would risk being swept away."

"We need a motor-boat," said Meaulnes, "or a steam launch like the one you had before."

"We no longer have it," she replied in a low voice, "we sold it."

And there was an embarrassed silence. Jasmin profited by it by announcing he was going to rejoin M. de Galais.

"I will know where to find him," he said. Bizarre chance! Two people so unlike each other and yet they had hardly been separated since morning. M. de Galais had taken me apart for a moment at the beginning of the afternoon to tell me I had in him a friend of great tact, deference and quality. Maybe, even, he had been on the point of confiding the existence of Belisaire to him, and his hiding-place.

I thought of leaving myself, but I felt the two young people were so awkward, so anxious, face to face with one another, that I judged it prudent not to.

So much discretion on the part of Jasmin, so much precaution on mine served little purpose. They talked, but with an obstinacy of which he was not aware, Meaulnes insisted on recalling all the marvels of former times. And each time the young girl had to repeat in agony that it had all disappeared; the strange old house demolished; the pond dried and filled in; the children in their charming costumes dispersed...

"Ah!" Meaulnes would say in despair as if each of the disappearances had proved him right in respect of the young girl or of me...

We walked along side by side. In vain I tried to create diversions from the sadness which was enveloping all three of us. With an abrupt question Meaulnes would return again to the same fixed idea. He asked for details about all that he had seen once before.....the little girls, the driver of the old berlin, the racing ponies.

"The ponies are also sold? There are no more horses at the domain? ...

She replied that there weren't any more there. She did not speak of Belisaire.

Then he remembered things in his room, the chandeliers, the long mirror, the broken lute...

He enquired about everything with a strange passion, as if he wanted to be persuaded that nothing now existed of his beautiful adventure, that the young girl could not salvage anything for him to prove they had not both dreamt it all, as the diver retrieves from the bottom of the sea a shell or some seaweed...

Mlle de Galais and I could not help smiling sadly; she decided to explain to him.

"You will not see the beautiful chateau again which M. de Galais and I had prepared for poor Frantz. We spent our lives fulfilling his desires. He was a strange being, yet so charming! But everything disappeared with him the evening his fiancée did not come. M. de Galais was already ruined without our knowing it. Frantz had piled up debts, and his old friends, learning of his disappearance, immediately claimed repayment from us. We became poor; Mme. De Galais died, and we lost all our friends in a few days. If only Frantz would return, if he is not dead, That he would find again his friends and his fiancée That the interrupted marriage would take place and all would return to what it once was. But can the past return? "

"Who knows?" said Meaulnes pensively. And he asked nothing more.

We walked silently, the three of us, on the short and slightly yellowing grass. Augustin had close to him on his right the young girl he had thought he had lost for ever. As he asked these cruel questions she would turn slowly towards him to reply. Her sweet face troubled, and once while speaking she put her hand gently on his arm in a gesture full of confidence and frailty. Why was big Meaulnes behaving like a stranger, like someone who has not found what he was looking for, and nothing else can interest him? Three years earlier he would not have been able to support this happiness without fear, without madness even. From whence came now this emptiness, this estrangement, the inability to be happy which preoccupied him now?

We were approaching the little wood where in the morning M. de Galais had tethered Belisaire. The sun was setting, lengthening our shadows on the grass. At the other end of the lawn we could hear, muffled by the distance, the happy buzz of voices of people playing and little girls, and we remained silent in this pleasant tranquility. Then we heard singing from the other side of the wood from the direction of the Aubiers. The farm was on the banks of the river. It was the young voice of someone in the distance bringing his animals to the water. It was a rhythmic tune like a dance tune, but the man was drawing it out to give it the languor of an old melancholy ballad.

"My shoes are red
Goodbye to my sweethearts
My shoes are red
Goodbye without return!"...

Meaulnes had lifted his head and was listening. It was one of the tunes sung by the unlettered peasants at the unknown domain the last evening of the fete when everything had already collapsed...a poignant reminder of those wonderful days which would never return.

"You hear it?" said Meaulnes in a low voice. "I'm going to see who it is." And straight away he set off into the little wood. Almost immediately the singing stopped. We could hear the man whistling to his animals in the distance; then nothing…

I looked at the young girl. Pensive and overwhelmed, her eyes were fixed on the thicket where Meaulnes had disappeared. How many times she was to watch thus pensively the road along which big Meaulnes would never come!

She turned towards me.

"He isn't happy," she said miserably. She added, "And perhaps can't do anything for him?"…

I hesitated to reply, fearing that Meaulnes who would have reached the farm In no time would now be retuning through the wood and surprise our conversation. But I was going to encourage her in the meantime, to tell her not to fear the brusqueness of the big boy, that there was a secret which was no doubt causing him to despair, and which he would never confide voluntarily to her or to anyone…When suddenly from the other side of the wood there was a cry. Then we heard stamping like that of a horse, interspersed with the sound of some dispute…I realized immediately that he had accidentally come upon old Belisaire and I ran towards the place from where the uproar was coming. Mlle de Galais followed me at a distance. Back on the lawn they must have heard the commotion for as I entered the thicket I heard the cries of people running.

Old Belisaire who had been tethered too low, had put one foreleg through his bridle; he had not moved until M. de Galais and Delouche, in the course of their walk, had approached him. Then disturbed and excited by the unaccustomed hay which they had given him, he had struggled furiously. The two men had tried to free him but so clumsily that they had succeeded in tangling him up further, even as they risked being struck by dangerous kicks from his shoes. It was at that moment that Meaulnes chanced to be returning from Ambiers' farm and came upon the group. Infuriated by so much ineptitude he had pushed aside the two men at the risk of sending them rolling into the bushes. Carefully but with one swing of his hand he had freed Belisaire. Too late, for the harm had already been done. The horse had sprained a ligament or maybe something had broken, for he hung his head down pitifully, his saddle half unstrapped on his back. He held up one leg under his stomach and trembled violently. Meaulnes was bent over and feeling and examining him silently.

When he raised his head almost everyone was assembled there but he did not see anyone. He was red with anger.

"I ask myself," he cried out "who on earth could have tethered him like this! And left the saddle on his back the whole day! And who had the nerve to saddle a horse which is good for no more than a light gig."

Delouche tried to say something and the blame fell on him.

"Be quiet! It's your fault anyway. I saw you pulling clumsily on his bridle to loosen him."

And bending over again he began to rub the horse's knee with the palm of his hand. M. de Galais who had not spoken so far made the mistake of breaking his silence. He stammered,

"Naval officers are accustomed to...my horse..."

"Oh, he's yours?" said Meaulnes a little calmed, very red as he turned his face to the old man. I thought he would alter his tone; make excuses. He breathed deeply for a moment, and I saw that he took a bitter and despairing pleasure in aggravating the situation, and destroying everything for ever, as he said rudely,

"Well I don't offer you my compliments." Someone suggested,

"Maybe some fresh water…if he's bathed in the ford..." Meaulnes said without answering,

"We have to take this old horse away immediately while he can still walk, and there is no time to lose! Put him in the stable and never take him out again."

Several young people offered straight away. But Mlle de Galais thanked them profusely, her face on fire and ready to burst into tears. She said goodbye to everyone, even to the embarrassed Meaulnes who dared not look at her. She took the animal by his reins as one gives someone one's hand, more to approach him gently than to lead him. The late Summer wind blew so mildly along the road to the Sablonniers that one could have believed it was May, and the leaves on the hedges trembled in the Summer breeze...Thus we watched them leave; her arm half extended from her cloak as she held the heavy leather rein in her right hand. Her Father walked painfully beside her....

A sad end to the party! Slowly everyone packed up his parcels and cloths. The chairs were folded and the tables put down. One by one the carriages full of luggage and people departed, hats raised and handkerchiefs waving. The last to leave, we remained in the field with my Uncle Florentin, who pondered like us, without saying anything, his regrets and his great deception.

We also left, carried speedily in our well-hung carriage, drawn by our beautiful chestnut bay. The wheel creaked as it turned in the sand, and soon Meaulnes and I who were seated on the bench at the back, saw the entrance to the path disappearing, the one which led to the Sablonnieres, the route taken by Belisaire and his Master and Mistress.

But then my companion – the being out of all the world I believed most incapable of weeping, turned towards me suddenly, his face devastated by a sudden rush of tears.

"Stop, will you please?" he said, putting his hand on Florentin's shoulder. "Don't worry about me. I will return alone on foot."

And in one bound, his hand on the mudguard of the vehicle, he jumped to the ground. To our amazement he turned back and began to run to the little path we had just passed from the Sablonnieres. He must have arrived at the domain by the fir-lined path he had followed once before when he had heard a vagabond hidden away among the low branches, and the mysterious conversation of beautiful unknown children...

And that evening, with tears in his eyes, he asked for the hand in marriage of Mlle de Galais.

7.   The Wedding Day

It is a Tuesday at the beginning of February, a fine frosty Tuesday afternoon and a great wind is blowing. It is half-past three, four o'clock ……..On the hedges around the towns the washing has been spread out since mid-day and is drying well. In each house the fire in the dining-room shines on a heap of varnished toys. Tired of playing, the child is seated close to his Mother and is asking her to tell him about her wedding-day…….

For anyone who does not want to be happy he has only to climb up to the attic and he will hear until the evening whistling and moaning as of shipwrecks. He has only to go outside on the road, and the wind will bring his silk handkerchief down on his mouth like a sudden warm kiss which makes him weep. But for anyone who likes happiness there is along a muddy road the Sablonnieres' house where my friend Meaulnes has returned with Yvonne de Galais who has been his wife since mid-day.

The engagement lasted five months. It was peaceful, as peaceful as the first meeting was turbulent. Meaulnes came very often to the Sablonnieres on a bicycle or in a carriage. More than twice a week while sewing or reading by the big window which overlooks the land and the fir trees, Mlle de Galais would suddenly see his tall silhouette passing quickly behind the curtain, because he came always by the same winding path he had taken the first time, but that is the only allusion –tacit – which he makes to the past. Happiness seems to have quietened his strange torment.

Little events made milestones during those calm five months. I was appointed teacher in the hamlet of Saint-Benoist-des-Champs. Saint-Benoist is not a village. There are scattered farms across the countryside, and the school-house is completely isolated on one side of the road. I lead a very solitary life; but by crossing the fields, it is only three-quarters of an hours' walk to the Sablonnieres.

Delouche is now with his Uncle who is a building-contractor in Vieux-Nancay. He will soon be the manager. He often comes to see me. Meaulnes on the pleading of Mlle de Galais is now very friendly with him. And this explains why we are both wandering about there towards four o'clock in the afternoon when the other guests have already left.

The marriage took place at mid-day in the greatest possible silence in the chapel of the Sablonnieres which had not been demolished and which the firs partially hid on a neighbouring slope After a quick lunch Meaulnes's Mother, M. Seurel and Millie, Florentin and the others climbed back into their carriages. There remained only Jasmin and myself............

We wander along the edge of the woods behind the Sablonnieres next to a large area of uncultivated land. This was the site of the old domain which is now demolished. Without wanting to admit it and without knowing why, we are full of a sense of foreboding. In vain we try to distract our thoughts and disguise our anxiety as we wander along aimlessly by pointing out to each other the tracks of hares and the little furrows in the sand which the rabbits have scraped out recently...a trap set...the traces of a poacher...But without pausing we return to the side of the thicket from where we can see the silent closed house...

Below the big window which looks out on to the fir trees there is a wooden balcony invaded by foolhardy grasses beaten down by the wind. A light as from a lighted fire is reflected on the window curtains. From time to time a shadow passes. All around in the surrounding fields, in the vegetable garden, in the one remaining farm left from the old tenancies, there is silence and solitude. The farmers have left for the town to celebrate the happiness of their masters. From time to time the wet wind dampens our faces and brings us the haunting note of a piano. Down below in the closed house someone is playing...I stop for a moment to listen in silence. At first it is like a trembling voice from far away which hardly dares to sing its joy...it is like the laughter of a little girl who in her own room has been getting out all her things and is spreading them in front of her friend...I am reminded also of the fearful joy of a young woman who has put on a beautiful dress and is going to show herself but does not know if she will please...that which I do not recognize is also a prayer, a supplication to happiness, not to be cruel, a salute or almost a genuflection before happiness...

I think, "They are happy at last. Meaulnes is down there near to her..."

And to know that, being sure of it, is enough for perfect contentment for the gallant child that I am.

At that moment, completely absorbed, my face dampened by the wind from the fields as by spray from the sea, I feel someone touch me on the shoulder.

"Listen," says Jasmin quietly.

I look at him. He signals me not to move; and he too, head inclined, listens...

8.   The Call of Frantz

"Hoo-oo!"

This time I heard it. It is a signal, an appeal on two notes, high and low, which I had already heard once before.......Ah! I remember; it is the cry of the great comedian when he used to call his young companion at the school gate. It is the call which Frantz made us swear to answer, no matter where, no matter when. But what did he want here today?

"It is coming from the big fir plantation to the left," I say quietly, "It is probably a poacher."

Jasmin shakes his head. "You know very well it isn't," he says. Then more quietly,

"They have been in this area, both of them, since the morning. I surprised Ganache at eleven o'clock busy digging in a field near the chapel. He ran off when he saw me. They have come a long distance by bicycle because he was covered with mud up to the middle of his back."

"But what are they looking for?"

"I don't know anything about that but we must definitely chase them away. We can't let them wander around here or all the follies will begin again…"

I am also of the same opinion without saying so.

"The best thing," I said, "will be to find them and see what they want and make them listen to reason..."

Slowly, silently, we slide through the thicket to the big fir plantation from where came at regular intervals the prolonged cry which was not of itself sadder than anything else, but which seemed to both of us to have a sinister intent.

It is difficult in this part of the fir wood where the trunks of the trees are planted regularly, and it is easy to see between them, to surprise someone without being seen .We do not even try. I stand at one corner of the wood. Jasmin places himself at the opposite corner, in order to command like me the exterior view of two sides of the rectangle and not allow the two bohemians to escape without calling them. This tactic in place I begin to play the soft role, calling out quietly,

"Frantz!..."

"Frantz! Don't be afraid. It's me, Seurel; I want to talk to you..."

"Stay where you are. I'll come and find you."

There is a moment of silence; I am about to call again, when, from the heart of the fir wood which my sight can not penetrate I distinguish the silhouette of a young man approaching. He seems to be covered in mud and poorly clad. Bicycle-clips hold in the bottoms of his trousers. An old anchor cap is placed on his long hair. I see now an emaciated figure. He seems to have been weeping.

Approaching me resolutely,

"What do you want?" he asks insolently.

"And you Frantz, what are you doing here? Why have you come to trouble those who are happy? What do you have to demand? Tell me."

Thus challenged directly he reddens a little, hesitates, and replies only,

"I am unhappy...I am very unhappy." Then his head in his arms, and leaning against a tree, he begins to cry bitterly. We have entered a few steps into the fir forest. It is absolutely silent. There is not even the sound of the wind which has been checked by the great fir trees at the edge of the wood. The sound of the stifled sobs of the young man echoes and is extinguished between the regularly planted trees. I wait for the crisis to pass and putting my hand on his shoulder, I say:

"Frantz, come with me. I will take you to them. They will welcome you like a lost child who has been found, and all will be well."

But he did not want to listen to me. In a voice muffled by tears, unhappy, obstinate, and angry, he repeated,

"So Meaulnes isn't bothered about me any more? Why didn't he reply when I called him? Why didn't he keep his promise?"

"Look Frantz," I reply, "the time for fantasies and childishness is over. Don't disturb the happiness of those you love, your sister and Augustin Meaulnes, with these follies."

"But only he can save me; you know that. Only he can find the tracks I am looking for. It is nearly three years since Ganache and I set off searching all over France, without result. My only hope is in your friend and he does not respond. He has found his love again. Why doesn't he think of me now? He must set off at once. Yvonne will let him go. She has never refused me anything."

He shows me a face in which tears have made streaks in the dust and mud, the face of an exhausted and beaten little old man. His eyes are surrounded by freckles; his chin is unshaven, his long hair falls on to his collar; his hands in his pockets, he trembles. This is no longer the royal child in rags of years gone by. At heart probably he is more of a child than ever: imperious, bizarre, and suddenly despairing. But this childishness is hard to bear in a boy who has already aged. Earlier he had had so much pride and youth that all the folly in the world seemed in him permissible. Now one was tempted at first to feel sorry that he had not succeeded in life...then to reproach him for his absurd role of the romantic hero in which he was so determined...and lastly I think, in spite of myself, how our fine Frantz of the great love affairs must have had to steal in order to live, just like his companion Ganache...so much pride has ended in this!

"If I promise you," I say after some reflection, "that in a few days Meaulnes will set off to fight for you, for no-one but you?..."

"He will succeed won't he? You are sure?" he asks me between chattering teeth.

"I believe so. Everything is possible with him."

"And how will I know? Who will tell me?"

"You will return here after exactly one year at the same hour, and you will find the young girl you love."

And in saying that, I plan not to trouble the newly-weds but to enquire myself from my Aunt Moinel, and try to find the young girl myself. The play-actor looks me in the eyes with a truly admirable desire to believe me. Fifteen years old, he was only fifteen years old when at Sainte-Agathe we had swept the classrooms one evening and had made, all three of us, this terrible childish vow.

Despair seizes him when he is forced to say, "Alright then, we're leaving."

He looks, certainly with a constriction of the heart, at the surrounding woods which he has to leave all over again.

"In three days we will be on the road to Germany," he says. "We left our vehicle a long way away, and have been walking for thirty hours without stopping. We expected to arrive in time to fetch Meaulnes before his marriage to come and look for my fiancée, as he looked for the Sablonnieres domain."

Then seized by a vicious childishness he says as he goes,

"Call your Delouche because if I meet him that will be terrible."

Gradually I see his grey silhouette disappear between the fir–trees. I call Jasmin and we resume our guard. But almost immediately we see Meaulnes close down the shutters of the house and are struck by the strangeness of his manner.

9.   The Happy People

Later I found out the details I write below.

From the beginning of the afternoon Meaulnes and his wife whom I still call Mlle de Galais remained completely alone in the drawing-room of the Sablonnieres. All the guests had gone. Old M. de Galais opened the door so that the strong wind penetrated the house for a second and moaned: then he set off towards Vieux-Nancay and would not return till the dinner hour to lock up and give orders at the farm. Now no more sound penetrated from the outside to disturb the young people. Only a branch of a rose-bush with no leaves tapped on the window which overlooked the land. Like two passengers in a drifting boat, in the great winter wind, they are two lovers enclosed in their own happiness.

"The fire is threatening to go out," said Mlle de Galais, and she wanted to take a log from the box.

But Meaulnes was there before her to put the wood on the fire himself.

Then he took the young girl's outstretched hand and they remained there facing each other, suffocated as by some great news which cannot be put into words.

The wind rolled around like the sound of an overflowing river. From time to time a drop of water crossed the window diagonally as on the window of a train.

Then the young girl left the room. She opened the door into the passage and disappeared with a mysterious smile. For a moment, in the half darkness Augustin remained alone...the tick-tock of a little pendulum reminded him of the dining-room at Sainte-Agathe...He thought probably: "This then is the house I searched for so long, with the corridor once full of whisperings and strange personages..."

It was at that moment that he must have heard – Mlle de Galais told me later as she also heard it – the first call of Frantz close to the house.

The young woman wanted to show him all the wonderful things she possessed: her childhood toys, all her childhood photographs: herself in baby-clothes - herself and Frantz on their Mother's knee.

She was so pretty. Then all that remained of her small sensible frocks of long ago, "until this one which I used to wear, see, about the time when you were soon to meet me, when you arrived I think for the course at Sainte-Agathe." Meaulnes was no longer attending and no longer listening.

Yet for a moment he seemed to be seized by the realization of his extraordinary unimaginable happiness.

"You are there," he said softly, as if only to say it made him feel dizzy – "you pass near to the table and your hand rests on it a moment..."

And,

"When my Mother was a young woman, she used to lean forward like that to talk to me, her breast almost on her waist...and when she began to play the piano..."

So Mlle de Galais suggested playing before it became dark, but it was already dark in the corner of the room and they had to light a candle. The pink from the shade increased the pink which already marked her cheek-bones and was the sign of some great anxiety.

On the edge of the wood I began to hear the trembling song brought to us on the wind, soon to be cut short by the cry from the two fools who were approaching us through the fir-trees.

For a long time Meaulnes listened to the young girl as he looked silently out of the window. Several times he turned towards the sweet face, so full of weakness and anguish. Then he approached Yvonne and very gently placed his hand on her shoulder. She felt the slight pressure of his caress near her neck and should have known to respond.

"It's getting dark," he said at last. "I'll close the blinds. But don't stop playing..."

What was going on in his obscure and savage heart? I asked myself many times, and found out only when it was too late. Stifled remorse? Inexplicable regrets? Fear that this unheard-of happiness which he grasped so tightly would soon disappear from between his hands? And then the terrible temptation to smash it to the ground, immediately, this marvelous thing which he had won?

He went out slowly and silently, after looking at the young woman's face one more time. We saw him from the edge of the wood closing a shutter hesitantly, then looking vaguely towards us as he closed the other. Then suddenly he set off at full speed towards us.... He reached us before we had time to think of any more dissimulation. He saw us as he was about to jump over a little hedge planted recently on the boundary of a field, and swerved. I remember his haggard appearance, his air of a hunted animal. He seemed to be going to return and jump the hedge on the other side of the little stream.

I called him:

"Meaulnes!...Augustin!...."

But he didn't even turn his head. So persuaded that this was the only way to stop him:

"Frantz is there," I cried, "Stop!"

He stopped at last. Panting and not leaving me time to prepare what I could say, he said,

"He is there! What does he want?"

"He is unhappy," I said, "He came to ask for help to find that which he has lost."

"Ah," he said, lowering his head, "I suspected as much. No matter how hard I tried to put that thought to sleep...But where is he? Tell me quickly."

I told him that Frantz had just left and that he certainly could not be reached again now. This was for Meaulnes a great disappointment. He hesitated, took two or three steps, and stopped. He seemed to be immobilised by indecision and regret. I told him what I had promised the young man in his name. I told him that I had arranged a meeting at this same place after a year. Augustin, usually so calm, was now in a state of extraordinary nervous impatience.

"Oh! Why did you say that!" he said. "Yes I can certainly save him. But it must be done immediately. I must see him and talk to him so that he will pardon me, and I can make reparation for everything. Otherwise I can no longer present myself down there..."

And he turned towards the Sablonnieres house.

"So," I said, "for a childish promise you made, you are about to destroy your happiness."

"Ah! If it were only that promise," he said.

And thus I knew that something else linked the two young men, but could not guess what.

"In any case," I said, "There's no point in running. They're now on the road to Germany."

He was going to reply when a disheveled haggard figure stood between us. It was Mlle de Galais. She must have run for her face was bathed in sweat. She must have fallen and hurt herself for her forehead was grazed above the right eye and there was clotting blood in her hair.

It happened once in the poor quarters of Paris that I saw a husband and wife suddenly came out fighting into the street. They were separated by others who tried to intervene in the quarrel. It was a household which was believed to be united, happy, and faithful. The scandal broke all of a sudden when they were sitting down to the table one Sunday to celebrate the birthday of the little son...and now all is forgotten. The husband and wife in the middle of the tumult are no more than two pitiful demons, and the children in tears are throwing themselves against them, hugging them tightly and begging them to be silent and stop fighting.

Mlle de Galais, when she reached Meaulnes, reminded me of one of those poor distracted children, one of those poor maddened distracted children. I believe that if all her friends, the whole village, the whole world were watching her she would have run just the same, that she would have fallen just the same, disheveled, weeping, grimed.

But when she realized that Meaulnes was still there, that this time at least he would not abandon her, she put her arm through his, and could not help laughing in the middle of her tears like a little child. They did not say anything, either of them. But when she had taken out her handkerchief Meaulnes took it gently from her hands: carefully and attentively he cleaned away the blood which stuck to the young girl's hair.

"We must go back now," he said.

And I let them return, the two of them, the fine strong wind of a Winter's evening whipping their faces, he helping her over the difficult places with his hand; she smiling and hastening – towards the home they had abandoned for a moment.

10. Frantz's House

Uneasy, and a prey to an obscure anxiety, which the happy ending to the turbulence of the day before had not succeeded in dissipating, I had to remain the whole of the next day confined to the school. As soon as the study hour which followed the evening classes was over I took the road to the Sablonnieres. Night was falling when I arrived at the path through the firs which led to the house. All the shutters were already closed. I was afraid of being inopportune in presenting myself at this late hour the day after a marriage. I remained for a long time prowling along the edge of the garden and in the neighbouring land, hoping all the time to see someone emerge from the closed house...But my hope was disappointed. Even in the neighbouring farm nothing moved. And I had to return home haunted by the gravest misgivings.

The next day, Saturday, the same uncertainty. In the evening I hastily took my cape, my stick, and a piece of bread to eat on the way, and I arrived when night had already fallen to find, as on the day before, everything closed at the Sablonnieres. There was a little light on the ground floor, but no sound; no movement...However from across the yard I saw that the farm door was open this time. The fire was lit in the big kitchen, and I heard the usual sounds of voices and footsteps at suppertime. This reassured me without enlightening me at all. I could not say anything or ask anything of these people. And I returned to watch again, to wait in vain, expecting all the time to see the door open and the tall silhouette of Augustin appear.

It was only on Sunday afternoon that I resolved to ring the doorbell at the Sablonnieres. As I climbed the bare slopes I heard in the distance the ringing of the bell for a Winter- Sunday vespers...I felt myself alone and desolate. I do not know what sad presentiment possessed me. And I was only half-surprised when at the ringing of the doorbell M. de Galais appeared all alone and spoke in a low voice; Yvonne de Galais had taken to her bed with a high fever; Meaulnes had left on Friday morning for a long journey. No-one knew when he would return...And as the old man was very embarrassed and unhappy, and did not invite me in, I took my leave immediately. After the door had closed I remained a few moments on the steps, my heart constricted and in a state of absolute helplessness, watching, I do not know why, a dry branch of wisteria sway sadly in a ray of sunlight.

Thus the secret remorse which Meaulnes had endured since his stay in Paris had eventually become too much for him. In the end my big companion had had to let go of his happiness…

Every Thursday and every Sunday I went to ask news of Yvonne de Galais until the evening when, convalescent at last, she asked me to enter. I found her seated by the fire in the drawing-room whose big low window looked out across the land and the woods. She was not pale as I expected. Rather she was in a fever, with vivid patches of red under her eyes, and she was in a state of extreme agitation…Although she was still very weak she was dressed as if to go out. She spoke very little but each phrase was uttered with extraordinary animation as if she wanted to persuade herself that her happiness had not vanished again...I do not remember what we said. I remember only that I had come to ask hesitantly when Meaulnes would return.

"I don't know when he will return," she replied feverishly.

There was supplication in her eyes and I was careful not to ask any more.

I returned often to see her. I would talk with her in front of the fire in the drawing-room where darkness fell more quickly than anywhere else. She never spoke of herself or her hidden pain. But she never tired of making me recite every detail of our lives as students at Sainte-Agathe.

She would listen gravely and tenderly, with an almost maternal interest, to the account of our woes as adolescents. She never seemed to be surprised even by the most audacious and dangerous of our childish follies. That attentive tenderness which she showed towards M. de Galais and to the deplorable adventures of her brother was never exhausted. The only regret for the past which moved her I think was of not being sufficiently in the confidence of her brother, since at the moment of his greatest debacle he had dared say nothing to anyone, feeling himself lost without appeal. And I realise now that this was a heavy burden the young woman had assumed. It was a dangerous responsibility to try to support a hysterical and fanciful spirit like that of her brother, and a crushing burden when it became linked with the adventurous heart of my friend big Meaulnes.

Of the faithfulness with which she guarded her brother's childish dreams; the care she brought to salvage for him at least some fragments of the fantasy world in which he had lived till the age of twenty, she gave me one day the most touching, and I would say even the most mysterious proof.

It was one April evening, desolate as the end of Autumn. For nearly a month we had been enjoying prematurely sweet Spring weather, and the young woman had resumed the long walks with M. de Galais which she loved. But that day, the old man being tired, and I myself free, she asked me to accompany her in spite of the threatening weather. A little more than half a league from the Sablonnieres we walked by the pond. A storm of rain and hail surprised us. As we stood close together under the shed during the interminable downpour, the wind freezing us as we pensively watched the darkening countryside, I saw her again in the same austere sweet dress, very pale and tormented.

"We must go back," she said, "we have been gone a long time. What might have happened?"

But to my astonishment, when it was possible to leave our shelter, the young woman, instead of turning towards the Sablonnieres, continued along the road and asked me to follow her. After having walked for a long time we arrived in front of a house which I did not recognize. It stood alone beside a road which must go towards Preveranges. It was a little bourgeois house with a slate roof and nothing much to distinguish it from the usual style of house in that area except for its loneliness and isolation.

To see Yvonne de Galais, one would have thought the house belonged to us and we had abandoned it for a long journey. She leaned over the little gate and opened it. Then ran to inspect the place with great anxiety. A large grassy yard where children must have come to play during the long Winter evenings had been ravaged by the storm. In the flower-beds where the children had sown flowers and peas the heavy rain had left only trails of white gravel. And then we discovered huddled against the doorstep of one of the wet doors a whole clutch of chickens drenched by the deluge. They were nearly all dead under the stiff wings and crumpled feathers of the mother.

At this pitiful sight the young woman gave a stifled cry. She bent down, and without a care for the water or the mud, she sorted out the live chickens from the dead and put them in a pocket of her cloak. Then we went into the house to which she had the key. Four doors opened into a narrow passage through which gusts of wind whistled. Yvonne de Galais opened the first on our right and invited me to enter the dark room. After a moment's hesitation I could distinguish a large mirror and a small camp-bed covered with a red silk eiderdown. She herself searched the rest of the house for a moment and returned with the sick brood tucked in a basket full of down. She slid it carefully under the eiderdown. And as a ray of sunlight, the first and last of the day, brightened our faces and made the darkness of the evening even darker, we stood there, frozen and tormented, in the strange house!

From time to time she went to inspect the feverish brood and remove any other dead chicken to prevent it infecting the others. And each time it seemed to us that something like a great wind penetrated the broken window-panes of the loft, like the mysterious grief of unknown children lamenting silently around us.

"This," my companion told me at last, "was Frantz's house when he was small. He wanted a house just for himself, far away from the rest of the world where he could come to play and amuse himself, and live whenever he pleased. My father found this fantasy so incredible and droll that he could not refuse him. And whenever it pleased him, a Thursday or a Sunday, no matter when, Frantz would go off to live in his house like a man. Children from distant farms used to come to play with him and help him keep house, or work in the garden. It was a wonderful game! And when evening came he was not afraid to sleep alone. As for ourselves, we admired him so much we never thought of being anxious."

"For a long time now," she continued with a sigh, "the house has been empty. M. de Galais, stricken by age and sorrow, has done nothing to control or reign in my brother. And what could he do?

"I come here often myself. The little peasant children from round about come to play in the garden as they used to do. And I like to imagine that they are the old companions of Frantz; that he himself is still a child and that he will soon return with the fiancée he has chosen.

"The children know me well. I play with them. This brood of little chickens was ours..."

It had taken this childish reversal and disaster for her to confide in me the great pain, the terrible grief, she had suffered at the loss of the brother who was so eccentric, yet so charming, and so much admired. And I listened silently, my heart overflowing with tears...

The doors and gate re-closed, the chickens returned to the wooden hut which stood behind the house, she took me arm again sadly, and I took her home.

Weeks and months passed. An era gone! Happiness lost! Of her who had been the fairy, the princess, the mysterious love, of our whole adolescence, it was on me fell the lot to take the arm and say whatever could be said to lighten the sorrow, while my companion fled. Of that time, of those evening conversations after the class which I took on the edge of Saint-Benoist-des-Champs, of the walks during which the only thing about which we should have talked was the one thing on which we had decided to remain silent, what could I say now? The only memory I have kept, half-blurred already, is of a fine emaciated face, two eyes whose lids lowered slowly as they looked at me, so as to see already only her own inner world.

And I remained her faithful companion – companion during a wait of which we did not speak – during the whole of that Spring and Summer, as if he would never come again. Several times we returned in the afternoon to Frantz's house. She would open the doors to let in the air so that nothing would be mildewed when the young householder returned. She busied herself with the half-wild birds which sheltered in the yard. And on Thursdays and Sundays we encouraged the little children of the countryside to come and play. And their cries and laughter in that solitary place made the little deserted house seem more empty, more abandoned than before.

11. Conversation in the Rain

The month of August, which was the vacation, distanced me from the Sablonnieres and the young woman. I had to go and spend the two months holiday at Sainte-Agathe…Everything spoke of Meaulnes. Everywhere was full of memories of our adolescence, now ended. During those long jaundiced days I shut myself up as in former times in the archives room, or in the deserted classrooms. My father would be off fishing. Millie was in the drawing-room sewing or playing the piano as before…And in the absolute silence of the classroom where the wreaths of torn green paper, envelopes, prize-books, cleaned boards, all said the year was over, the prizes distributed, everything waiting for the Autumn, the return of October and the new effort…I thought anew that our youth was over and happiness had passed us by. I waited for my return to the Sablonnieres and the return of Augustin who might never return…

There was meanwhile a new happiness to announce to Millie when she decided to question me about the newly married couple. I dreaded her questions and the manner in which, at once innocent and yet malicious, she would put her finger on my most secret thoughts. I cut everything short by announcing that Meaulnes' wife would be a mother in October.

On my own part I remembered the day Yvonne had given me to understand the great news. There had been silence; on my part the slight embarrassment of a young man. And in order to dispel it I had said immediately, remembering too late how disturbed she would be,

"You must be very happy?"

But she, without a backward thought, regret, rancour or remorse, had replied with a beautiful smile of happiness,

"Yes, very happy."

During that last week of the holidays which was usually the lovely and romantic week of the great rains, when we began to light fires again, and which I usually spent hunting among the dark wet pines of Vieux-Nancay, I made my preparations to return directly to Saint-Benoist-du-Champs. Firmin, my Aunt Julie, and my cousins from Vieux-Nancay asked too many questions I did not wish to answer. I renounced this time the eight invigorating days of hunting in the countryside, in order to return to my school-house four days before the commencement of classes.

I arrived before nightfall in the school-yard which was already covered in yellow leaves. The driver left. I unpacked sadly in the echoing and solitary dining-room. My mother had given me a parcel of provisions ...After a light and hasty meal, impatient and anxious, I put on my cloak, and left for a feverish walk which took me to the boundary of the Sablonnieres.

I did not wish to intrude by presenting myself there the first evening of my arrival. However, more bold than I had been in February, I walked round the whole domain where only one light shone in the young woman's own window. Then I jumped over the garden fence behind the house and sat on a bench close to the bridge in the evening darkness, happy simply to be there close to what excited and disturbed me more than anything in the world. Night came. A fine rain began to fall. Head lowered, I contemplated without thinking about it my shoes getting slowly wet, and shining in the water. Darkness encompassed me and the freshness of the air blew round me without disturbing my reverie. Tenderly, sadly, I dreamed of the muddy roads that same September evening in Sainte-Agathe; I imagined the place full of mist, the butcher-boy as he walked slowly along in his pumps, the lighted café, the joyful carriage with its' canapé of open umbrellas arriving before the end of the holidays at my Uncle Florentin's...And I said sadly to myself: what does all that happiness matter when Meaulnes, my companion, cannot be there, nor his young wife...

It was then that, raising my head, I saw her, two steps away. Her shoes in the sand had made a gentle sound which I had confused with that of drops of water from the hedge. She had a black woolen shawl round her head and shoulders and the rain had powdered the front of her hair. No doubt she must have seen me from the window which looked out on to the garden. And she had come to me. Thus once my mother had grown anxious and come looking for me to tell me to come in. Then having enjoyed the walk in the rain and darkness had simply said gently, "You will catch cold," and remained in my company to talk a while...

Yvonne de Galais gave me her burning hand, and abandoning the idea of inviting me into the Sablonnieres, sat on the driest side of the wet and mouldy bench, while I stood, resting my knee on the same bench, and leaning towards her to hear her.

She scolded me first, amicably, for having thus cut short my holiday.

"It was necessary," I replied, "to come early to keep you company."

"It is true," she said quietly with a sigh, "that I am still alone. Augustin has not come back..."

Taking her sigh to mean regret, I stifled a reproach. I began to say slowly,

"So much folly in so noble a head! Maybe the taste for adventure which was stronger than anything..."

But the young woman interrupted me. And it was in this place, that evening, for the first and last time, that she talked to me about Meaulnes.

"Don't say that," she said gently, "Francois Seurel, my friend. It is only we, it is only I myself who am guilty. Think what we have done...We told him, here is your happiness, here is what you were searching for all your youth, here is she who is the fulfillment of all your dreams! When we pushed him thus between the shoulders, must he not have been seized with hesitation, then fear, then fright, and yielded to the temptation to run away!"

"Yvonne," I said quietly," you know very well that you were that happiness, that young girl."

"Ah," she sighed, "how could I have held that proud thought for an instant! It is that belief which has been the cause of everything. I would say to you, 'suppose I can't do anything for him.' And inwardly think, 'since he has searched for me for so long, and since I love him, it must be that I am his happiness.' But when I saw him close to me with all his fever, his anxiety, his mysterious remorse, I realized I was only a poor woman like any other..."

"I am not worthy of you," he kept saying when it was dawn and the end of our wedding night. And I tried to console him, to reassure him. Nothing could calm his distress. Then I told him,

"If it is necessary for you to go, if I have come to you at a moment when nothing can make you happy, if it is necessary for you to abandon me for a while, in order to return later at peace, then it is I myself who ask you to go..."

In the darkness I saw that she had raised her eyes to mine. It was like a confession she had made to me, and she waited anxiously to know whether I approved her or condemned her. But what could I say? Certainly in my heart I could see Meaulnes as he had been, awkward and wild, taking punishment rather than excusing himself; refusing to ask a permission he knew would be granted. No doubt Yvonne would have had to commit a violence by taking his hand in hers and saying, "It doesn't matter what you have done. I love you. Aren't all men sinners?" But certainly she had done him a great wrong in her generosity and spirit of sacrifice, by thrusting him out again on his road of adventure. Yet how could I disapprove such goodness, such love! ...

There was a long moment of silence, during which, distressed to the depths of our hearts, we listened to the cold rain trickling through the hedges and under the branches of the tress.

"So he left in the morning," she continued. "Nothing would ever separate us again. And he embraced me simply like a husband who leaves his wife before a long journey..."

She rose. I took her feverish hand in mine, then her arm, and we went back up the path in the darkness.

"Yet he never wrote to you?" I asked.

"Never," she replied.

And then, the thought coming to both of us of the adventurous life he was leading now along the roads of France or Germany, we began to speak of him as we had never done before . Forgotten details, old impressions restored to our memory, as we slowly approached the house, pausing at each step, the better to exchange our recollections...For a long time, as far as the boundaries of the garden, in the dark I listened to the precious low voice of the young woman; and I, overtaken by my old enthusiasm, talked to her tirelessly, with profound friendship, of him who had abandoned us...

12. The Burden

School was to recommence on Monday. The Saturday evening towards five o'clock a woman from the domaine entered the schoolyard where I was sawing wood for the Winter. She had come to announce that a little girl had been born at the Sablonnierres. The confinement had been difficult. At nine o'clock at night it had been necessary to send for a midwife from Preveranges. At midnight they had had to reharness to search for the doctor in Vierzon. He had had to use forceps. The little girl's head was damaged and she cried a lot, but she seemed to be thriving. Yvonne de Galais was in a state of collapse but she had endured the pain with extraordinary bravery.

I left my work, ran to put on my coat, and satisfied on the whole with these tidings I followed the woman to the Sablonnieres. Carefully, for fear of disturbing the sleep of one of the two sufferers, I climbed the wooden steps which led to the first floor. And there, M. de Galais, his face tired but happy, invited me into the room where a crib surrounded by curtains, had been temporarily installed.

I had never entered a house where a baby had been born the same day. How strange and mysterious and good did this one seem! It was such a lovely evening, a real Summer's evening, that M. de Galais was not afraid to open the window on to the yard. Leaning beside me on the window-sill he recounted with both distress and happiness, the drama of the night, and I who listened felt obscurely that there was a stranger with us in the room...

Behind the curtains she began to cry, a little bitter and prolonged cry... The M. de Galais told me in a low voice,

"It's the wound on her head which makes her cry."

Mechanically – one got the impression that he had been doing it since morning and had developed the habit – he began to rock the little curtained basket.

"She has laughed already," he said, "and she takes a finger. But you haven't seen her."

He opened the curtains and I saw a little red bundled figure with a skull elongated and deformed by the forceps.

"That's nothing," said M. de Galais. "The doctor said all that will come right on its own...Give her your finger. She will grasp it."

I discovered there a new world. I felt my heart swell with a strange joy that I had not known before...

M. de Galais quietly opened the door to the young woman's room. She was not asleep.

"You can go in," he said.

She was stretched out, her face fevered in the middle of her scattered blond hair. She held out her hand to me with a languid smile. I congratulated her on her daughter. With a slightly hoarse voice and unusual coarseness, the coarseness of one who has returned from a battle, she said smiling,

"Yes, but I was forced to wound her."

It was necessary to leave her then in order not to tire her.

The next day, Sunday, in the afternoon, I set off with an almost joyful haste to the Sablonnieres. On the door a notice fixed with pins stopped my hand which was already raised:

"Please do not ring the bell."

I could not understand what was the matter. I knocked loudly. I heard shuffling steps running inside. Someone I did not know, who was the doctor from Vierzon, opened the door.

"What's going on?" I cried.

"Shh!" he replied quietly in a distraught manner. "The little girl nearly died in the night, and the mother is very sick."

Completely bewildered, I followed him on tiptoe up to the first floor. The little girl asleep in her crib was very pale, as white as a little dead child. The doctor expected to save her. As for the mother he could not say anything...He gave me long explanations as to the only friend of the family. He spoke of pulmonary congestion and embolism. He hesitated, he wasn't certain...M. de Galais entered. He had aged dreadfully in two days and was trembling and haggard.

He took me into the room, hardly knowing what he was doing. He told me,

"She mustn't be frightened. I had to tell the doctor to persuade her all is well."

Her face on fire, Yvonne de Galais was spread out with her head thrown back as on the night before. Her cheeks and forehead were dark red. Her eyes rolled back for a moment like someone who was suffocating. She fought death with indescribable sweetness and courage.

She could not speak but she held out her hand to me with so much friendship that I almost burst into tears.

"Well, well," said M. de Galais very loudly with a dreadful playfulness which sounded idiotic. "You see that for a sick person she does not look too bad."

And I did not know how to reply, but I kept the dying woman's fiery hand in mine...

She wanted to try to tell me something, to ask I do not know what. She turned her eyes towards me, then towards the window, as if to ask me to look outside for someone....But then a frightening crisis of suffocation took hold of her; her beautiful blue eyes which for a moment had appealed to me so tragically rolled back; her cheeks and forehead turned black and she struggled gently, striving to control to the end her terror and despair. Everyone rushed, the doctor and the women, with an oxygen balloon, towels, flasks, while the old man leaned over her crying, shouting as if she had already gone a long way from us, in a gruff trembling voice.

"Don't be afraid Yvonne. It is nothing. There's no need to be afraid."

Then the crisis passed. She could breathe a little but she continued to be half-suffocated, her eyes white and her head back, struggling all the time, but unable, even for a moment, to look at me and speak, or return from the gulf into which she had already plunged.

And as I was no use I decided to go. No doubt I could have remained a moment longer; and at that thought I am seized by a terrible regret. But why? There was still hope. I persuaded myself that the end was not so near.

As I arrived at the edge of the fir-wood behind the house, remembering the way the young woman had looked towards the window I peered intently into the wood like a guard or a watchman in the direction from which Augustin had once come and by which he had fled the previous Winter. Alas! Nothing moved, no suspicious shadow, no branch. But in the distance below, in the direction of the road which came from Preveranges, I heard very faintly, a little bell. Soon around the bend appeared a child wearing a red cap and a school smock, following a priest. And I left, swallowing my tears.

The next day was the beginning of the school term. At seven o'clock there were already two or three boys in the yard. I hesitated a long time to go down and show myself. And when I appeared at last, turning the key of the mildewed classroom which had been closed for two months, I saw the biggest of the schoolboys detach himself from the group playing under the shelter and approach me. He came to tell me,

"The young lady at the Sablonnieres died yesterday at nightfall."

Everything is in confusion for me, everything drowned in sorrow. It seems to me now that I will never have the courage to begin the class. Simply crossing the schoolyard is an exertion for me, causing my knees to ache. Everything is painful, everything bitter because she is dead. The world is empty, the holidays finished. Finished the lost journeys in a carriage, finished the mysterious fete...everything becomes the struggle which it had been before.

I told the children there would be no class that morning. They left in little groups taking this news to others who were crossing the countryside. As for me, I took my black hat, a trimmed jacket which I have, and set off miserably to the Sablonnieres...

...Here I am before the house for which we searched for three years! It is in this house that Yvonne de Galais, wife of Augustin Meaulnes, died last night. A stranger would mistake it for a chapel, such is the silence in this desolate place since yesterday.

There then was what had been stored for us, that fine first day of term, and the treacherous Autumn sun slides through the branches. How I struggled against this frightening revolt, the suffocating mounting of tears! We had found the beautiful young girl. We had conquered. She was the wife of my companion and I loved her with a profound and secret friendship which I never told. I would look at her and be content like a little child One day perhaps I would have married some other young girl, and it would have been to her, the first, to whom I would have confided the great secret...

Near the bell at the corner of the door, yesterday's notice has been left. The coffin has already been brought into the hall downstairs. In the first-floor room it is the children's wet-nurse who welcomes me, who tells me about the end, and who gently opens the door...Here she is. No more fever, no more struggle, no more redness, no more waiting...Nothing but silence, and surrounded by cotton-wool, a hard face, insensible and white, a dead forehead on which lies the hard thick hair.

M. de Galais, crouched in a corner with his back towards us is in socks without shoes, and he is digging with a dreadful obstinacy into drawers, all in disorder, which he has dragged from their chest. From time to time with an attack of sobbing which shakes his shoulders like a burst of laughter, he takes out some old yellowed photograph of his daughter.

The burial is to be mid-day. The doctor fears the rapid decomposition which sometimes follows an embolism. This is why the face, like all the rest of the body, is surrounded by cotton-wool soaked in formalin.

The dressing completed - they have put her in a lovely dark blue velvet dress scattered in places with silver stars, though they must have had to iron and crimp the beautiful leg-of-mutton sleeves which are now old-fashioned - they are now going to bring the coffin upstairs, but have discovered they can not turn the coffin in the narrow stair-case. They will have to hoist it up on a rope through the window, and in the same way lower it down again.....But M. de Galais, still leaning over his old things amongst which he searches for, one knows not what lost souvenirs, intervenes with terrible vehemence,

"Rather," he says in a voice broken with tears and anger, "rather than allow such a dreadful thing, I will carry her myself downstairs in my arms..."

And he would have done it, at the risk, in his weakness, of falling half-way down, and collapsing with her.

But then I step forward to do the only thing possible. With the help of the doctor and a woman, passing my arm under the back of the dead girl and the other under her legs, I hold her against my chest. Seated on my left arm, her shoulders leaning on my right arm, her head turned towards me under my chin, she weighs terribly on my heart. I go slowly, step by step, down the steep stair-case while everything is prepared below.

My arms are breaking with fatigue. At each step, with the weight on my chest, I am a little more breathless, clutching her inert and heavy body. I lower my head on to the head of her who I am carrying. I breathe heavily and her blond hairs enter my mouth – dead hairs which have the taste of earth. This taste of earth and death, this weight on the heart, is all that remains to me of the great adventure, and of you, Yvonne de Galais, young woman so much searched for – so much loved…

13. The Monthly Homework Exercise-Book

In that house, so full of sad memories, and where women rocked and consoled the little sick baby all day, old M. de Galais soon took to his bed. At the first severe cold of Winter he died peacefully, and I could not help weeping by the bedside of the charming old man whose indulgent fancy, allied with that of his son's, had been the cause of all the adventure. He died very happily in complete forgetfulness of all that had happened, and in almost complete silence. As for a long time he had had neither relatives nor friends in that part of France, he had made me executor of his entire legacy until the return of Meaulnes. I would give an account of everything to him if he ever returned...And so it was at the Sablonnieres that I lived henceforth...I no longer went to Saint-Benoist except to take the classes, leaving early in the morning, dining at mid-day on a meal prepared at the domain and heated on the school stove, and returning in the evening immediately after school. In that way I could keep close to the infant whom otherwise the servants were looking after. Above all I would have a better chance of meeting Meaulnes if he returned one day to the Sablonnieres.

I did not despair of finding in the end in the cupboards or drawers of the house some paper or indication of how he had spent his time during the long silence of the previous year, and perhaps thereby discover the reason for his flight, or at least some hint of his whereabouts...I had already searched I don't know how many cupboards and wardrobes in vain. From the cabinets in the lumber-room I unearthed a quantity of ancient boxes of all shapes, which turned out to be full of old letters and yellowed photographs of the de Galais family, packed along with artificial flowers, feathers, aigrettes, and other old-fashioned trifles. From these boxes emanated I don't know what ancient odour, what faint perfume, which awoke in me suddenly and for the rest of the day, memories and regrets and brought an end to my search...

Then, one holiday, I noticed a small old box in the attic. It was long and shallow and covered with a threadbare pig-skin, and I recognized it as being Augustin's when he was a student. I reproached myself for not having started my search here I snapped the rusty lock open easily The box was full to the top with exercise-books, and books from Sainte-Agathe – arithmetic, literature, exercise-books full of problems – didn't I know it all? With emotion rather than curiosity I began to rummage through them, re-reading dictations I still knew by heart. We had copied them out so many times! Rousseau's "L'Aqueduc", "Un Aventure en Calabre" by P.-L Courier, "Lettre de George Sand a son Fils"...

There was also an exercise-book for monthly homework. I was surprised to see it because these exercise-books normally remained in the school, and the pupils never took them outside. It was a green exercise-book, yellowing round the edges. The name of the pupil, "Augustin Meaulnes" was written on the cover in a magnificent circle. I opened it. From the date of the homeworks, April 189- I saw that Meaulnes had begun it a few days before leaving Sainte-Agathe. The first pages were written with the religious care which was the rule when we worked in these composition books. But no more than three pages were written on. The rest was blank and that was why Meaulnes had taken it away with him. As I reflected, kneeling on the floor, on the customs and childish rules which had occupied such a large part of our adolescence, I lifted the edges of the unused pages with my thumb. And it was thus that I discovered the writing on the other pages. After leaving four pages blank he had begun to write.

It was still Meaulnes's writing, but rapid and ill-formed, hardly readable; small paragraphs of unequal size separated by blank lines. Sometimes there would be incomplete phrases. Sometimes a date. For the first time I guessed that I could have here information on the time Meaulnes had passed in Paris, and indications of the track I was seeking. I went down to the dining-room to read the strange document in the daylight. I was a clear windy Winter's day. Sometimes bright sunlight cast shadows of the window-panes on the white curtains; sometimes a sharp gust cast an icy blast against the panes. And it was near that window in front of the fire that I read the lines which explained so many things, and of which this is an exact copy.......

179

14. The Secret

"I have passed under the window once again. The glass is still dusty and whitened by the curtain behind it. If Yvonne de Galais should open it I would have nothing to say to her for she is married...What can I do now? How can I live?....

Saturday 13th February: I met the young girl on the embankment where I met her the previous June, waiting like me in front of the closed house...I talked to her. As she walked I observed out of the corner of my eye the small faults in her face: a little line at the corner of her mouth, a slight hollowing of the cheek, and powder caked round the nostril. She turned suddenly and looked me full in the face - maybe because she is more beautiful full-face than in profile - and said briefly,

"You amuse me a lot. You remind me of a young man who courted me once in Bourges. He was even my fiancé..."

However that evening she approached me in the dark on the deserted wet pavement which reflected the light from the gas-lamp, and asked me to take her to the theatre that night with her sister...I noticed for the first time that she was dressed in mourning in a hat too old for such a young girl, and carried a long umbrella like a cane. And as I was close to her and made some gesture my finger-nails caught the crepe of her blouse...I made difficulties about agreeing to her request. She was annoyed and wanted to leave immediately. And now it was I who kept her and begged. A labourer passing by in the pleasant darkness said softly,

"Don't go my dear. He will do you some harm."

And we stood there, the two of us, struck dumb.

At the theatre: the young girls, my friend who is called Valentine Blondeau, and her sister, arrived in poor finery. Valentine was placed in front of me and constantly turned round anxiously as if to ask what I wanted of her. And I, close to her, felt almost happy, and responded each time with a smile.

All around us there were ladies whose dresses were cut too low and we made jokes. It was she who smiled first and then said,

"I should not laugh. I am also too décolleté." And she wrapped herself in her scarf. In fact under the square of black lace, one could see that in her haste while changing clothes she had turned down the top of her high-necked blouse.

There is in her look a combination of poverty and childishness; a curious mixture of suffering and bravado which attracts me. Near to her, the only person in the world who could have told me something about the people in the mysterious domain, I never cease to think of that strange adventure.....I wanted to ask her again about the little hotel in the boulevard, but she in turn asked me such embarrassing questions that I did not know how to reply. I think that in future we will both be silent on the subject. And yet I also know that I will see her again. To what purpose? And why?...Am I not condemned now to follow in the tracks of anything which bares the scent, however faint, however distant, of my lost adventure?...

At midnight, alone in the deserted road, I wonder what this new and strange story means for me. I walk along in front of the houses like a line of cardboard boxes, in which everyone is asleep. And I suddenly remember a decision I had made the previous month. I had resolved to go there at night, around one o'clock in the morning, to look around the hotel, to open the garden gate and enter like a thief, and search for some sign which would lead me to the lost domain, just to see it again, only to see it...But I am soon tired. I am hungry. I had also hastened to change my clothes for the theatre, and I had not dined...Restless and uneasy I remain sitting on the edge of my bed for a long time before sleeping, a prey to a vague remorse. For what cause?

I noted this again: They did not want me to take them home, nor to tell me where they lived. But I followed them as far as I could. I know they live in a little road which turns towards Notre-Dame. But what number?...I guessed they were dress-makers or milliners.

To avoid her sister, Valentine arranged to meet me on Thursday at four o'clock in front of the same theatre where we went before.

"If I am not there tomorrow," she said, "meet me on Friday at the same hour, then Saturday, and continue the same every day."

Thursday 18th February: I have come to wait in a strong, rain-bearing wind. I expect rain at any moment.

I walk in the semi-darkness of the roads, a weight on my heart. A drop of water falls. I fear that it will start to rain: a shower will prevent her coming. But the wind takes up again and the rain still does not fall. Up above in the grey afternoon sky – grey and bright in turn – a large cloud must have given way to the wind. And I am fixed here, miserably waiting.

In front of the theatre: After quarter of an hour I am certain that she will not come. From the pavement where I am, I stare into the distance to the point where she would have come, and in the passing crowds I watch all the young girls in mourning that I can see, and I feel almost an aquaintanceship with those who resemble her the longest as they approach me and give me hope...

An hour of waiting: I am tired. At night-fall a guardian of the peace takes to the neighbouring post a ruffian who in a stifled voice hurls at him all the insults, all the obscenities that he knows. The officer is furious, pale, silent...From the entrance he begins to beat him. Then he closes the door on us to beat the poor man at his ease. There comes to me the frightening thought that I have renounced Paradise, and I am at the gates of Hell.

Worn out, I leave the place and regain this narrow lane between the Seine and Notre-Dame where I know somewhere their house is situated. Alone I walk to and fro. From time to time a servant or a housewife comes out in the light rain to do her shopping before dark...There is nothing here for me and I leave...I return in the clear rain which holds back the dark, and pass by the place where we were to have met. There are more people than a short while ago; a black crowd...

Suppositions – despair – fatigue – I am supported by the thought of tomorrow. Tomorrow at the same time, at the same place, I will come again to wait. And I am in great haste that tomorrow should come. Wearily I think of the evening and tomorrow morning which have to pass unemployed...But isn't today almost finished?...At home, close to the fire, I hear the vendors calling the names of the evening papers. No doubt somewhere in the town in her lost house near the Notre-Dame she also hears them.

She...that is to say...Valentine.

That evening I wanted to be over weighs on me strangely. While the clock moves slowly towards the time when today will be over and I wish already finished, there are people who have invested in it all their hope, all their love and their last efforts. There are men who are dying; others expecting bankruptcy, and wish tomorrow would never come. There are others for whom tomorrow will dawn with remorse. Others are tired and tonight will not be long enough to give them all the rest they need. And I, I who have lost my today, by what right dare I call for tomorrow?

Friday evening: I expected to write as a conclusion, "I did not meet her again". And everything would have been finished. But on arriving this afternoon at four o'clock at the corner of the theatre she was there. Slender and grave, dressed in black but with powder on her face and a little collar which gives her the air of a guilty pierrot. An air which is at the same time doleful and mischievous. She has come to tell me that she will leave immediately and will never return…

And yet at nightfall we are still walking slowly close together on the gravel by the Tuileries. She tells me her story, but in such a cryptic fashion that I misunderstand her. She said, 'my lover' in speaking of her fiancé whom she had not married. She did it purposely, I think, to shock me and so that I would not become attached to her.

These are phrases of hers which I write out:

"Don't put any confidence in me," she says, "I have never done anything but stupidities."

"I have walked the roads all alone."

"I despaired of my fiancé. I abandoned him because he admired me too much; he saw me only in his imagination and never as I really was. For I am full of faults. We would have been very unhappy."

All the time I felt her to be making herself out to be worse than she was, I think to prove to herself that she had been right to commit the folly of which she speaks, and that she had nothing to regret, and she was not worthy of the happiness which was offered to her.

Another time:

"What I like in you," she told me after looking at me for a long time, "what I like in you, I can't understand why, are my memories."

183

Another time:

"I love him still," she would say, "more than you think."

And then suddenly, brusquely, brutally, sadly,

"Anyway. What do you want? Do you love me too? Are you going to ask for my hand as well?..."

I stammered. I don't know how I replied. Maybe I said, "Yes."

This manner of journal was interrupted here. Then there began drafts of letters, illegible, ill-formed, half-erased. Precarious engagement!.....The young girl, on the request of Meaulnes, abandoned her trade. He himself was occupied with the marriage arrangements, but never ceasing in his desire to search again, to set off again on the trail of his lost love. He must have disappeared several times; and in his letters, with a tragic embarrassment, he tried to justify himself to Valentine.

15. The Secret (continued)

Then the journal was resumed. He recorded a stay they made in the country, the two of them, I don't know where. But it was a strange thing to do at that time. Perhaps because of secrecy the journal was written in such an incoherent and haphazard fashion. And scribbled so hastily also, that I have had to re-write it myself and reconstruct all this part of the story.

14th June: When we woke that morning in the bedroom in the inn, the sun had lit up the red pattern on the black curtain. Farm labourers in the room below were talking loudly while drinking their morning coffee. They were complaining in rough peacable tones against their employers Meaulnes had probably heard the even sound for some time in his sleep because he took no notice o0f it at first. The curtain strewn with clusters of grapes reddened by the sun, the sound of morning voices coming up into the silent room; all this contributed to the typical impression of a morning in the country at the beginning of a delicious long holiday.

He got up and knocked on the neighbouring door, and not getting any response, he opened the door quietly. Then he saw Valentine and understood the cause of his quiet happiness. She was asleep, absolutely still and silent. Even her breathing could not be heard, as a bird must sleep. For a long time he looked at her childish face with its eyes closed, a face so quiet that one would have wished never to wake her or trouble her again.

She made no other movement to show that she was no longer asleep than to open her eyes and look up at him.

As soon as she was dressed Meaulnes returned to the young girl.

"We are late," she said.

And immediately she was like a housewife in her home.

She tidied the two rooms, brushed the clothes Meaulnes had worn the day before, and when she came to the trousers she was grieved that the lower parts of the legs were covered in thick mud. She hesitated, then carefully, before brushing, she began to remove the top layer of the mud with a knife.

"The boys in Sainte-Agathe," said Meaulnes, "did like that when they fell into the mud."

"It was my mother who taught me this," said Valentine

And so good did the countryside feel, which before his mysterious adventure must have taken to its heart the hunter and peasant who was Meaulnes.

15th June: At that dinner on the farm, where thanks to the friends who had introduced them, they were entertained to their embarrassment as husband and wife, she behaving timidly like a bride.

The candles were lit in two candelabras at each end of the table which was covered with a white cloth as at a simple country wedding. The faces as they leaned forward were shadowed under the feeble light.

Valentine sat to the right of Patrice (the farmer's son), then Meaulnes, who remained silent till the end even though people talked almost entirely to him. Since in this lost village, to avoid inviting comment, he had let Valentine pass as his wife, he was haunted by the same regret, the same remorse. And while Patrice, after the fashion of a country gentleman, presided over the dinner, Meaulnes was thinking,

"It is I who this evening, should be in a dining-room like this, a beautiful room which I used to know well, presiding over my own marriage feast."

Next to him, Valentine refused timidly all that was offered to her. She behaved like a peasant girl. At each new approach, she would look at her friend and seem to seek refuge against him. For a long time Patrice insisted in vain that she drink her wine, till at last Meaulnes leaned towards her and said gently,

"You should drink, my little Valentine."

The docilely she drank. And Patrice, smiling, congratulated the young man on having such an obedient wife.

But the two of them, Meaulnes and Valentine, remained silent and pensive. For one thing they were tired. Their feet, soaked in the mud after their walk, were frozen on the scrubbed flag-stones of the kitchen. And then, from time to time, the young man was obliged to say,

"My wife, Valentine, my wife..."

And each time, as he pronounced this word in a muffled voice, in front of the unknown peasants in the dark room, he had the impression of committing a fault.

17th June: The afternoon of that last day began badly. Patrice and his family accompanied them on a walk. Gradually on an uneven slope covered with bracken, the two couples found themselves separated. Meaulnes and Valentine sat down among some juniper trees in a little copse.

The wind carried drops of rain and the sky was overcast. The evening had left a bitter taste, it seemed to him, the taste of such boredom that even love could not distract him.

They stayed there for quite some time in their sheltered hiding-place under the branches, speaking little. Then the weather cleared, and it was fine. They thought then that all would be well.

And they began to speak of love. Valentine talked and talked...

"This is what my fiancé promised me," she said, "like the child that he was. All of a sudden we would have a house, like a cottage hidden in the country. It is quite close, he would say. We would arrive there like travelers from a long journey on the eve of our marriage, about this time, close to nightfall. And along the lanes, in the yard, hidden in the groves, unknown children would greet us crying, 'here comes the bride!' What foolishness, wasn't it?"

Meaulnes, dumbfounded, concerned, listened to her. He rediscovered in all this, the echo of a voice already heard. And there was also, in the young girl's tone as she told this story, a vague regret.

But she was afraid of having wounded him. She turned to him with warmth and sweetness.

"To you," she said, "I want to give everything that I have: something which has been to me the most precious of all...And you are jealous!"

Then, looking at him anxiously, she took out of her pocket a little packet of letters which she handed to him, the letters of her fiancé.

Ah! Immediately he recognized the fine writing. Why had he never thought of this sooner! It was the writing of Frantz, the play-actor, which he had seen once in the desperate note left in the bedroom of the Domain...

They were walking now along a narrow path between daisies and the hay, lit obliquely by the five o'clock sun. Meaulnes was so stunned that he could not grasp what sort of reverse this signified for him. He read because she asked him to read. Childish phrases, sentimental, pathetic...This came in the last letter:

"Ah! You have lost the little heart, naughty little Valentine. What will happen to us? Anyway I am not superstitious..."

Meaulnes read, half blind with regret and rage, his face immobile but very pale, with a twitching under his eyes. Valentine, distressed to see him like this, looked at where he had reached to see what was upsetting him so much.

"That," she explained very quickly, "was a jewel which he had given me, making me swear to keep it always. It was one of his mad ideas."

But she succeeded only in exasperating Meaulnes.

"Mad!" he said, putting the letter in his pocket. "Why do you repeat that word? Why did you never believe in him? I knew him. He was the most marvelous boy in the world!"

"You knew him," she said in an extremity of emotion, "you knew Frantz de Galais?"

"He was my best friend, he was my brother in adventure, and here I have taken his fiancée!

"Ah!" he went on furiously, "what harm you have done to us, you who wanted to believe in nothing. You are the cause of everything. It is you who have lost us everything! Everything!...."

She wanted to speak to him, take his hand, but he repulsed her brutally.

"Go away. Leave me alone."

"Alright. If it's like that," she said, her face on fire, listening and half-weeping. I'll go. I shall go back home to Bourges with my sister. You know, don't you, that my father is too poor to keep us. And if you don't come to look for me I will leave again for Paris and walk the streets as I did once before. I shall certainly become a lost woman because I no longer have any trade..."

And she left to collect her baggage and catch the train, while Meaulnes, without even watching her go, continued to walk at random.

The journal was interrupted again.

There followed more incoherent scarps of letters, the letters of a man who was undecided, astray. On returning to La Ferte-d'Angillon Meaulnes wrote to Valentine, apparently to tell her his resolution never to see her again and to give her precise reasons, but in reality, maybe, so that she would reply. In one of these letters he asked her what, in his derangement it had not occurred to ask her before, if she knew where the lost domain was that he had searched for so long.....In another he begged her to seek reconciliation with Frantz de Galais. He would take responsibility for finding him,...All these letters in which I saw the disorder of his mind, must not have been sent. But he must have written two or three times without receiving any reply. It was for him a period of extreme conflict and misery in absolute isolation. He must have felt his great resolution slowly weaken. And after the pages which follow - the last of the journal - I imagine one fine morning he must have hired a bicycle to go to Bruges to visit the Cathedral.

He left very early by the beautiful straight road through the woods, inventing on his way a thousand pretexts to present himself with dignity, without asking for reconciliation, before her whom he had driven away.

The four last pages which I could reconstruct tell of the journey and the last mistake.

16. The Secret (conclusion)

25th August: On the other side of Bruges at the edge of the new suburbs, he found, after searching a long time, the house of Valentine Blondeau. A woman, Valentine's mother, on the doorstep, seemed to be waiting for him. She was a fine figure of a woman, heavy and untidy, but beautiful still. She watched him curiously as he approached, and when he asked if Valentine Blondeau was at home she explained to him gently that they had returned to Paris on the 15th of August.

"They didn't tell me where they were going," she added, "but if you write to the old address the letters will be forwarded."

As he retraced his steps across the garden, his bicycle in his hand, he thought,

"She is a party to it...Everything is finished as I wanted it to be...It is I who forced her to this. 'I will certainly become a lost woman', she said. And it is I who forced her to it. It is I who have lost Frantz's fiancée!

And, ridiculously, he said quietly to himself, 'So much the better! So much the better!' Knowing that on the contrary it was so much the worse. Before the woman's eyes, before he reached the gate, he stumbled and fell on his knees.

He did not think of taking breakfast, but stopped at a café where he wrote a long letter to Valentine, for no reason except to deliver himself of the desperate cry which was stifling him. His letter repeated over and over again, "You could have...you could have...you could have relinquished all THAT! You could have lost yourself THAT way!"

Near to him some officers were drinking. One of them recounted noisily a story of a woman. He could hear it in scraps: "...I told her....you must know me better....I spend every evening with your husband!" The others laughed, turning their heads to spit behind their benches. Pale and dusty, Meaulnes watched them like a beggar. He imagined them taking Valentine on their knees.

After a long time he cycled round the Cathedral, saying to himself obscurely, "After all I came to see the Cathedral." Beyond the roads, on a vacant area, he saw it rising enormous and indifferent. These roads were narrow and dirty like the roads which surround village churches. There were occasional brothels with red lanterns. Meaulnes felt their sadness, lost in this unclean and vicious quarter for the lost, as in ancient times, under the buttresses of the Cathedral. He was visited by a peasant's fear, a repulsion, for this town church where all the vices were sculpted in its niches, built amongst bad places, and having no remedy for the purest sorrows of love.

Two girls were just passing, their arms round each others' waists and looking at him boldly. Out of disgust, or for fun to take revenge on his love, or to despoil it, Meaulnes followed them slowly on his bicycle. One of them, a miserable girl whose blond hair was drawn behind into a false chignon, told him to meet her at six o'clock in the Archbishop's garden, the garden where Frantz, in one of his letters, had arranged a meeting with poor Valentine.

He did not say no, knowing that by that time he would have left the town long ago. And from her window in the sloping street, she remained a long time, signaling to him vaguely.

He hastened back to the road.

Before leaving he could not resist a dreary wish to pass for a last time in front of Valentine's house. He stared hard at it, stocking himself up on misery. It was one of the last houses of the suburb, and the road turned out to be one by which he could leave the place....In front the land formed a sort of little square. There was no-one at the windows, nor in the yard, nor anywhere. Only two boys in rags dawdled along by the wall. A dirty powdered girl passed by.

It was here that Valentine had spent her childhood, here that she had begun to look at the world with trusting wise eyes. She had worked and sewn behind those windows. And Frantz had come here to see her, to smile at her, in this suburban road. But now there was nothing, nothing....and Meaulnes knew only that in some lost place, that same afternoon, Valentine was seeing in her memory this sad place where she would never return.

The long return journey which lay before him must be his last defense against pain, his last forced distraction, before he was entirely drowned in it.

He left. Along the road, in the valley, beautiful farm-houses under the trees and beside the streams displayed pointed gables decorated with green trellis-work. No doubt on their lawns young girls talked earnestly about love. He could imagine their souls, their beautiful souls.....

But for Meaulnes at that moment, there existed only one love, one poorly satisfied love which was being stifled so cruelly, and the young girl whom above all he should have protected and safe-guarded, was the girl he had sent to perdition.

A few hasty lines in the journal showed me that he had decided to find Valentine at all costs before it was too late. A date in the corner of a page suggested that this was the long journey for which Mme. Meaulnes was making preparations when I arrived at La Ferte-d'Angillon and upset everything. In the abandoned town-hall Meaulnes was writing his diary and jotting down his plans for one fine morning at the end of August, when I had brought him the great news for which he was no longer waiting... He was surprised, immobilized, by his old adventure, not daring to do anything or promise anything. Then began the remorse, the regret, and the pain, sometimes stifled, sometimes triumphant, until the wedding-day when the cry of the play-actor from among the fir-trees had recalled him theatrically to his first oath as a young man.

In the same monthly homework exercise-book he had scribbled some hasty words at dawn before leaving with the permission – yet for always – of Yvonne de Galais, his wife since the day before:

"I am leaving. I have to find the trail again of the two play-actors who came yesterday into the fir-wood and left towards the East on their bicycles. I will return to Yvonne only if I can bring with me and install in Frantz's house, Frantz and Valentine married.

This manuscript which I began as a secret journal, and which became my confession, will be, if I do not return, the property of my friend Francois Seurel.

He must have slipped the exercise-book hastily under the others, and turned the key of his old student's box, and disappeared.

Epilogue

Time passed. I lost hope of ever seeing my companion again and dreary days slid by in the country school, sad days in the deserted house. Frantz did not come to the meeting-place I had fixed with him, and my Aunt Moinel no longer knew where Valentine lived.

The only joy at the Sablonnieres was the little girl they had been able to save. By the end of September she even proved to be a strong and pretty little girl. She would soon be a year old. Fastened to the bars of chairs she would push them all by herself as she tried to walk, without caring about her falls, and she made a noise which reawakened after a long time the muted echoes of the abandoned domain. When I took her in my arms she never let me give her a kiss. She had a style which was at once wild, but charming, of wriggling and beating my body, with shouts of laughter. With all her gaiety and baby violence one felt she would chase away the sorrow which had reigned in the house since her birth. I would say to myself sometimes,

"No doubt in spite of her wildness she will be partly my child." But once again Providence dictated otherwise.

One Sunday morning at the end of September I had risen very early, even before the servant who looked after the little girl. I was going fishing in the Cher with two men from Saint-Benoist and Jasmin Delouche. Often villagers from the surrounding countryside would accompany me on grand poaching parties: fish in our hands in the dark, prohibited fishing-nets...Throughout the Summer in all weathers we set off at dawn and did not return till mi-day. It was the livelihood of almost all those men. As for myself, it was my sole pastime, the only escapade to replace the adventures of former times. And I had ended up developing a taste for these excursions along the river or in the reeds of the pond.

That morning I was standing in front of the house at five-thirty under a little shelter, leaning on the wall which separated the English garden of the Sablonnieres from the cottage garden belonging to the farm. I was busy disentangling my nets which I had thrown in a heap the previous Thursday.

Daylight had not yet come. It was the dawn-light of a fine September morning, and the shed where I had thrust my tackle in haste was still in the dark.

I was there, busy and quiet, when I suddenly heard the gate opening; a step sounded on the gravel.

"Oh ho," I thought, "here are my people earlier than I had expected, and here I am not ready!"...

But the man who entered the yard was unknown to me. He was, as far as I could make out, a large bearded fellow dressed like a hunter or poacher. Instead of coming to look for me there, where the others knew I always was at that time, for our meeting, he went straight to the door.

"Good," I thought, "it's one of their friends they have invited without telling me, and they will have sent him as a scout."

The man rattled the latch gently without making a noise. But I had locked it as I left. He made as if to go round to the kitchen entrance. Then, hesitating for a moment, he turned towards me, clear now in the half-light, his bearing anxious. And it was only then that I recognized big Meaulnes. For a long moment I remained there, afraid, desperate, gripped by all the sorrow which his return had reawakened. He had disappeared behind the house, and having done the tour, returned hesitating.

Then I advanced towards him, and without saying anything embraced him with tears. Immediately he understood.

"Ah!" he said briefly. "She's dead isn't she?"

I took him gently by the arm and led him towards the house. It was daylight now. Immediately, to get the worst over, I made him climb the staircase which led to the room of the death. As soon as he entered he fell on his knees beside the bed and for a long time rested his head in his arms.

He rose at last, his eyes crazed, staggering, not knowing where he was. And still guiding him by the arm I opened the door which communicated with the little girl's room. She had woken up alone while her nurse was below, and deliberately sat up in her crib. We caught her surprised look as she turned towards us.

"Here is your daughter," I said.

He gave a jump and stared at me.

Then he seized her and lifted her up in his arms. He could not see her at first as he was weeping. Then as a small distraction from the emotion and flow of tears, all the while holding her tightly against him, he turned towards me, and said,

"I have brought them, the other two...You can go and see them in their house."

And when morning broke, pensive and almost happy, I went to Frantz's house, which Yvonne de Galais had once showed me empty. From a distance I could see a young housewife, wearing a ruff, sweeping the doorstep, and object of curiosity and enthusiasm for several little cow-herds dressed in their Sunday best on their way to mass...

Meanwhile the little girl became bored with being held thus tightly, and as Augustine, his head leaning to one side to hide and stop the tears, still did not look at her, she gave him a big slap with her little hand on his bearded wet mouth.

This time the father lifted her high up, and tossed her at arms' length, and looked at her with a laugh. Satisfied, she clapped her hands...

I moved slightly to see them better. A little disappointed and yet amazed, I realized that the little girl had found at last here the companion she had been waiting for obscurely...the only joy which big Meaulnes had left me. I well knew he had returned to take her away from me. And already I imagined him one night wrapping up his daughter in a cloak, and setting off with her for new adventures.

Printed in Great Britain
by Amazon